'Frankly, Tilly,' Jandy said briskly, 'as far as I'm concerned the new registrar can look like Godzilla the ape as long as he can do the job.

'Unless he can patch someone up who's been in an RTA and send them home better than they came in, I can assure you that a whole team of rugby-playing registrars dressed only in their birthday suits wouldn't interest me…'

Tilly swivelled her eyes to look at the door behind Jandy and widened them slightly, then she gave a little giggle. 'Oops!' she muttered.

Jandy whirled round and reddened. 'Oh...er, hello,' she said lamely to the tall, broad man who stood in the doorway. She was conscious of a strong patrician face and dark blue eyes looking into hers, one eyebrow raised quizzically.

Trust her to make a fool of herself, she thought ruefully. A flustered glance at the man confirmed that with his formidable physique he was definitely the sort who would like roaring round a rugby pitch on a wet Saturday afternoon, or pounding the streets in an invigorating daily run. He was almost certainly the new registrar, and he looked every inch the super-confident hotshot doctor from London!

Dear Reader

Writing about Jandy and Patrick was kick-started by a conversation with a friend of mine. She'd been a single hard-working mum, with no time in her life for romance, and after years of putting her child first had lost confidence in going out on a date with anyone. She did meet her dream man in the end, quite unexpectedly, and this inspired me to write about Jandy, who has given up all hope of meeting a soul-mate but, despite her busy multi-tasking life, finds him eventually.

It was great fun to write, and I was quite sorry to say goodbye to Jandy, Patrick and their little girls at the end of the book! I do hope you enjoy reading it.

Best wishes

Judy

FROM SINGLE MUM TO LADY

BY
JUDY CAMPBELL

MILLS & BOON®

First published in Great Britain 2010
Harlequin Mills & Boon Limited,
Eton House, 18-24 Paradise Road, Richmond, Surrey TW9 1SR

ISBN: 978 0 263 21499 4

Harlequin Mills & Boon policy is to use papers that are natural,
renewable and recyclable products and made from wood grown in
sustainable forests. The logging and manufacturing process conform
to the legal environmental regulations of the country of origin.

Printed and bound in Great Britain
by CPI Antony Rowe, Chippenham, Wiltshire

CHAPTER ONE

'OH, NO! What the...?' yelped Jandy Marshall, as a freezing cascade of water poured down on her, soaking her hair and nurse's uniform in a few traumatic seconds. She stared up at the kitchen ceiling and the ever-widening circle of damp in disbelief and groaned. 'Not that damn pipe...it's burst again!'

Just what she needed on a Monday morning, she thought bitterly, scrabbling under the sink for the stop tap and shoving a bucket under the steady stream of water. She grabbed a tea towel from a drawer and towelled her hair before stepping out of her clothes and throwing them into the sink. She was getting quite adept at coping with disasters like this—if it wasn't the pipe bursting, it was the washing machine having a nervous breakdown...

She picked up the phone and dialled the plumber's number from memory, watching as the pouring water became a trickle and then an intermittent drip.

'This is an out-of-hours service. Your call is important to us, and we will be with you as soon as possible...'

Jandy slammed down the phone and glared at it aggressively. It seemed the rest of the world needed a plumber as well...she'd have to leave it for the time being.

As Monday mornings went, it hadn't been a good start. Apart from the burst pipe, there was a load of white washing which had been transformed to a uniform bright pink. Jandy loved Lydia dearly, they were as close as twin sisters could be, but sometimes she could strangle her when she was being extra-scatty instead of just ordinarily inefficient: colouring all the washing indeed! And trust her to still be nicely tucked up in bed after a late night while everything was going haywire downstairs!

'What's the matter, Mummy? Are you cross? You're very wet!' Four-year-old Abigail looked with interest at her mother's expression and then at the soaking floor.

Jandy sighed—cross was an understatement! What she really felt was very tired. She hadn't had a holiday in ages and life seemed to be all work and no play. She loved her work in the A and E department of Delford General but it would have been nice to go out socially occasionally.

She smiled ruefully down at her daughter. 'The pipe's burst again, and your red dress was washed with all the white things and now it's coloured everything else pink.'

'I like pink,' said Abigail placidly.

Jandy laughed. 'Well, that's all right, then!'

And of course what did a few discoloured garments matter when she might be losing the little house she rented? The final straw that morning had been the letter from the estate agent saying that the owner wanted to sell the property, but she could have first refusal if she was interested in buying.

No chance of that at the moment, thought Jandy, grimacing as she slung the sheets over the line in the kitchen. Paying for child care, a car, and just general living seemed to soak up most of what she earned. They'd just have to look around for another rented property—but she'd never find anything as good as the house they were in, or as reasonably priced.

Surely the day couldn't get any worse. She flicked a look at her watch and sucked in her breath—she had a quarter of an hour to put on a fresh uniform and get to the hospital after dropping Abigail off at the childminder's—she might just do it.

Jandy felt the familiar flash of guilt as she rushed back down the path after a hurried hug of farewell when she'd taken her little daughter to Pippa's. She always seemed to be at the last minute, playing catch-up and, she reflected wryly, clearing up after her sister. She turned as she closed the gate and looked back to see Abigail waving at her from the window, looking perfectly happy. She was adorable and Jandy was so lucky to have her…she just wished there was a father on hand to complete the picture…

The clock was nudging 8.05 a.m. as she parked her car in the last space of the hospital staff car park, ran up the steps and clattered through Reception on her way to the locker room.

Danny Smith, the receptionist, looked up from his lads' mag and shook an admonitory finger at her. 'You'd better hurry up…his lordship's showing the new registrar round the department now.'

Damn—she'd forgotten there'd be a new person on the staff today, someone else to get used to and have to guide for a while. She'd been wrong about the day not getting any worse, she thought irritably as she pulled on her hospital greens. No doubt about it, she could feel a bad mood coming on. Of course she couldn't begrudge Sue taking six months' maternity leave, although she was going to miss her terribly and the fun they had. When she was feeling down, Sue would cheer her up with a joke or a teasing comment: she was a kindred spirit, and life at Delford General was going to be that much duller now without her. What she needed, thought Jandy, pulling her blonde hair back into the ponytail she wore for work, was a bit of excitement—something new to revitalise her and brighten up the everyday humdrum. And the chances of that happening at the moment were more remote than winning the lottery.

The man stood for a moment before the entrance to the A and E department looking up at the square new wing that had been attached to the old Victorian hospital. He was a tall figure, the collar of his jacket turned up against the cold, and head and shoulders above the people swirling around him. So here he was—back where he'd been born, starting over again and picking up the pieces of his life. Soon London would become a distant memory, and Delford was going to be his home once more…his and Livy's, and he'd just have to make the best of it.

Straightening his shoulders as if bracing himself for his new life, he picked up the briefcase by his feet and started to make his way purposefully through the automatic doors into the A and E waiting room. He glanced briefly at some parents and two small children in one corner, and a man in a wheelchair gazing at a television on the wall showing a quiz show. Evidently the rush hadn't yet started.

'Patrick Sinclair—locum registrar for A and E checking in,' he said to the man behind the glass window in Reception.

* * *

The staff for the daytime shift were in the kitchen, all grabbing a drink before the day started in earnest and some crisis erupted. Tim Vernon, the dapper little A and E consultant, was walking briskly out of the room as Jandy came in. Two junior nurses were gossiping and Bob Thoms, one of the registrars, was peering at the duty roster, an anxious frown creasing his brow—he was a great worrier. He turned round as Jandy came in.

'Oh, great—what a relief, you're here! I thought you might be ill or something and we'd be short-staffed!' he exclaimed. 'You OK?'

'A burst pipe, no plumber and water all over the place,' she said gloomily. 'Worst of all I've had notice that the landlord wants to sell the house. Marvellous start to a Monday.'

Sister Karen Borley, large and kindly, handed her a cup and smiled at her sympathetically—she knew Jandy's mornings were a little chaotic and that she was only ever late if there'd been an emergency of some kind.

'Here you are, my girl—this'll perk you up.' She looked sympathetically at Jandy. 'You'll be looking for somewhere else to live, then—I'll keep my eyes open.'

Jandy took a gulp of scalding coffee and closed her eyes gratefully. 'Ah, thanks, Karen, you're a pal. Umm, that coffee's good… I'm coming round a bit now.' She turned to the others. 'Tell me, what's this new reg like?'

'He looks capable, although I think Tilly might find another adjective.' Karen laughed. 'He's from one of the big London teaching hospitals and has a wonderful CV, so he should be sound enough.'

'I hope he's easy to work with,' Jandy said mournfully. 'It won't be the same without Sue.'

'If I know anything about these hot-shot doctors from down South, he'll have an ego as big as an elephant and an inflated idea of his ability,' commented Bob Thoms tetchily.

A picture of Terry, Abigail's father, floated into Jandy's mind—he had been a high-flying business man from London who had felt demeaned coming up further north than Watford Junction! Jandy had mistaken his arrogance for a kind of sophisticated confidence and had been immensely flattered by his attention—she'd been easily taken in. She wouldn't be fooled a second time, but the thought of working with another person like that was not a comforting one.

'So coming up to Delford will be small time to him, I suppose,' she sighed. 'I wonder why he's come?'

'We'll get used to him,' said Karen, picking up some files and walking towards the door. 'I'll see you in a few minutes for the handover from the night shift—I'm just off to check that the porter's put the waste bins round the back. You come with me, Valerie,' she added to one of the student nurses. 'I'll show you where I like my supplies kept—I can't bear mess.'

Tilly Rodman, the other student nurse, rolled her eyes as Karen and Valerie went out. 'I can't believe that sister said the new reg is only "Capable"! He's gorgeous! My blood pressure went up like a rocket when I saw him...'

Bob Thoms drained his coffee and sighed. 'I'd like to know what this man has that I haven't...'

He left the room, but not before his eyes met Jandy's in amused exasperation. Tilly fell in love regularly with the senior registrars even if they looked only half-human. She would be in ecstasies about him for weeks, convinced that this was The One, as she put it on the many occasions she fell for someone.

Tilly had yet to learn, thought Jandy wryly, that looks weren't everything. In her experience handsome didn't always mean kind or thoughtful—sometimes it disguised selfish and cruel.

She rinsed her mug under the tap and dried it vigorously with a tea towel. What on earth did she know about men anyhow? It had been so long since she'd been out on a date—everyday life had taken over and any offers were quickly rebuffed. After Terry all her confidence had gone where relationships were concerned—she didn't want to be hurt again and her priority now was little Abigail. Anyway, her sister had enough assurance when it came to men for both of them!

'Frankly, Tilly,' she said briskly, as she folded the towel neatly and hung it on a rail, 'as far as I'm concerned, the new registrar can look like Godzilla as long as he can do the job. Unless he can patch someone up who's been in an RTA and send them home better than they came in, I can assure you that a whole team of rugby-playing registrars dressed only in their birthday suits wouldn't interest me...'

Tilly's eyes swivelled to look at the door behind Jandy, and widened slightly, then she gave a little giggle. 'Oops!' she muttered.

Jandy whirled round and reddened. 'Oh...er, hello,' she said lamely to the tall, broad man who stood in the doorway. She was conscious of a strong patrician face and dark blue eyes looking into hers, one eyebrow raised quizzically.

Trust her to make a fool of herself, she thought ruefully. A flustered glance at the man confirmed that with his formidable physique he was definitely the sort who would like roaring around a rugby pitch on a wet Saturday afternoon or pounding the streets in an invigorating daily run. He was almost certainly the new registrar, and he looked every inch the super-confident hot-shot doctor from London, as Bob Thoms had put it!

His gaze flickered over her in a mildly interested manner, taking in her slightly flushed cheeks and wide dark brown eyes.

'I don't normally turn up for work in a birthday suit,' he remarked blandly. 'But I do play rugby and I hope I can send the patients home in fairly good shape!'

He had a deep attractive voice—'well bred' was the expression that sprang to mind.

Jandy allowed herself a prim smile, and said in a dignified tone, 'I'm just trying to explain to Tilly here that expertise is more important than anything…'

'Of course, I couldn't agree more,' the man said, nodding gravely. 'I'm Patrick Sinclair, by the way—taking over from Sue Gordon. I was told that there might be some coffee going if I was lucky.'

His sudden smile took her by surprise, rather like the sun coming out from a cloud, and it lit up his whole face. He looked almost boyish and, Jandy supposed grudgingly, was reasonably good looking. She noticed a faded white scar that ran down the side of one cheek—the result of a rugby tackle, she imagined, and when he turned on the smile Jandy could easily understand why Tilly had fallen for him. But how would she feel if she discovered he had a wife and three children?

Jandy held her hand out to him and said rather stiffly,

'Welcome to Delford General, then. I'm Staff Nurse Jandy Marshall, and this is Tilly Rodman, one of our student nurses.'

He turned to Tilly dipping his head slightly. 'Ah, yes—we met before, I think. I'm looking forward to working with you.'

Tilly gulped and stared at him admiringly. 'Yeah... great...'

'Perhaps a cup of coffee for Dr Sinclair,' prompted Jandy with a touch of impatience.

Tilly looked as if she was rooted to the spot by the sight of this man—surely all the women in Casualty weren't going to buckle at the knees as soon as they saw him, Jandy thought irritably. She flicked another look at Patrick Sinclair—he was just another locum registrar passing through the department for a few months, a stopgap until Sue returned. OK, so he looked rather like a marketer's dream for advertising some quasi-medical cure for flu— she supposed deep blue eyes in a strong good-looking face could easily persuade gullible people to buy a product...

She frowned: Patrick Sinclair had the confident air of someone who knew how attractive he was—but he was here to do a job, not act as the department's pin-up! As a single mum juggling motherhood and a demanding job, she certainly wasn't going to pander to his self-importance.

Karen Borley put her head round the door. 'Tilly—can you come to the plaster room, please, and do a bit of clearing up—the place is a tip.'

'Yes, Sister.' Tilly thrust a cup of coffee into the man's hand and bolted out of the room, with a final blushing look at Patrick, and Jandy was left alone with him.

In the short silence between them Jandy caught a depressing sight of herself in the mirror over the sink. She didn't look her best—as usual her hair was scraped back into a ponytail to keep it off her face, and she hadn't a scrap of make-up on. If only she'd put on a touch of lipstick it might have made her look less severe, less pallid, instead of which she looked what she was: an overworked single mum who'd been multi-tasking since she'd got up that morning! Not that it mattered what Patrick Sinclair thought of her looks, she told herself sharply. Nevertheless, she drew herself up to her full five feet six inches, and sucked in her stomach.

'Have you had a tour of the department yet?' she asked Patrick.

'Not yet. Dr Vernon was called away and didn't have time to show me much.'

He took a sip of coffee and for the first time she noticed the broad band of gold on his left ring finger. So he was married—a crushing blow to Tilly and probably every woman in Casualty, thought Jandy wryly. Well, she certainly wasn't going to start moping because he was a married man, even though she had to admit that he was the first blazingly attractive male to have worked in A and E for ages—which didn't mean she had to start thinking of love, romance or any sort of attachment. The last sort of man she needed was another hot-shot guy from the cosmopolitan life in London who found himself in the northern sticks of England and was married—she'd been there, done that.

He smiled at her. 'So you and I are going to be colleagues—have you been at Delford General long?'

'About three years now—I enjoy it really, most of the time. Where have you been working?'

'In London, at S. Cuthbert's. It's a good hospital—I've

been there since I qualified, but the last six months I've been with the London Air Ambulance for a stint.'

Jandy was impressed despite herself—this guy had some pretty comprehensive experience in trauma, and you had to have nerves of steel to cope with the serious accidents you dealt with on a daily basis.

'Won't you miss that? It could seem quite dull here!'

He laughed. 'I don't think so—I might miss the good things about London, like the river, the Houses of Parliament, all the theatres...'

Suddenly a picture flashed into her mind of him in a theatre foyer, dressed immaculately in a dinner jacket, with a gorgeous woman on his arm, an easy, sophisticated confidence about him—leading the kind of life that she could only dream of.

'I expect,' she said challengingly, 'you'll find us old-fashioned after a place like St Cuthbert's.'

He looked at her quizzically, detecting her defensive tone, and remarked lightly, 'I'm sure I won't—most hospitals have similar procedures, don't they?'

'But what on earth made you come up to Delford?' Jandy asked rather bluntly. 'It sounds as if you had a wonderful life in London.'

'My father isn't too well and I need to be nearer him,' he explained. 'There's a lot of sorting out to be done which I can't do from London.'

Although he probably wishes he wasn't here in boring Delford, which could boast a cinema and not much else, surmised Jandy, but she felt a little ashamed of her unwelcoming thoughts and said more gently, 'I'm sorry about your father—that's a worry for you, and of course it must have been a wrench to leave your exciting life in London.'

Was it her imagination, or did a fleeting glance of sadness cross his face, something indefinable that hinted that life hadn't been that wonderful in London after all? However, when he spoke his voice was light.

'Yes—I was very happy there...but life here will have its own advantages, I'm sure. I came from this area originally, and there's some beautiful countryside around that I'm looking forward to exploring again and showing to my daughter. I'm coming back to my roots, you might say.'

'That'll be fun,' said Jandy politely.

'And you?' he enquired. 'Have you always lived and worked in Delford?'

Jandy nodded. 'Most of the time. I did leave for a short while and went to Manchester.' She paused for a second, then started wiping the draining board fiercely. Funny how even after all this time just the thought of the place sent a shock wave of horror through her mind. Then she turned back to him with a tight smile and said briefly, 'It didn't work out how I thought it would, so I came back.'

She tried to hide her feelings, but those warm brown eyes of hers couldn't disguise the fact that something pretty awful had happened to her there, reflected Patrick. Funny—she looked like a golden girl that had everything going for her—soft fair natural looks and a healthy, curvaceous figure—who would have thought that there were any ghosts in her past? But he'd obviously touched a raw nerve there, he guessed, something that she wanted to forget...just like him, just like millions of people.

'And you live in Delford now?'

'Probably not for long,' sighed Jandy. 'I've just been told

we've got to get out of the house we're in—a pity, because it's so near the childminder and shops. I doubt if we'll find anywhere else so convenient—or so reasonably priced. There's a small college in the town and all the good places get snapped up pretty quickly.'

'I hope something turns up,' Patrick said politely.

'Oh, I'll get something,' said Jandy brightly, pushing away the horrible worry that she might not have a roof over her head in a month's time. 'And now perhaps I can give you a quick tour of the delights of Delford General A and E before we get cracking.'

Patrick looked at Jandy with interest as he followed her out of the room—so she had a child as well. For some reason he'd imagined her to be a free agent, but just because she had no wedding ring it didn't mean she was unattached. He felt a momentary stab of disappointment, the reflex emotion of a hot-blooded male to a stunning woman who was already in a relationship, then shrugged inwardly. Speculating on a social life was the last thing he needed at the moment—looking after his father and little daughter would absorb all his time, and of course getting heavily involved with someone could be very dangerous, as he'd learned to his cost. At least, he reflected, there was help on hand now to look after Livy when she wasn't at school, and she would have a lovely home and gardens to play in.

Jandy having shown him the layout of the theatres and X-ray department, they went back to the central station where computers monitoring the stage of every emergency patient's treatment flickered and changed as the results of tests came through. On the wall behind the large curving desk were the whiteboards that listed which cubicle each patient was in, with a short résumé of their condition. A gradual building up of activity in the department had started, and a steady flow of patients was waiting to be seen by the triage nurse. In the background a child wailed from one of the cubicles in the paediatric section and a man was arguing loudly with the receptionist in the waiting room.

'I thought this would happen,' said Bob Thoms mournfully as he went off to one of the cubicles to examine an abscess on someone's back. 'I was hoping to get some new tyres from that garage opposite if we got ten minutes off for lunch, but it looks as if it's going to be solid patients wall to wall.'

Tim Vernon, immaculate in his white coat and neatly knotted tie, came up to Patrick. 'Sorry to leave you just then, Patrick, but you'll soon get the hang of things, I'm sure, after all your experience in London. Anyway, it's good to have you in the department—and I bet your father is delighted you've come back here to live with him. That place of his is far too big for one person. Tell him I miss our games of golf.'

So he'd moved his family in with his father, thought Jandy, standing near them as she flicked through the admissions chart. She wondered idly whereabouts in Delford Patrick's father lived and smiled wryly. There was no chance of Abigail, her sister and herself moving in with her widowed mother while she was looking for a new place— her mother lived in a tiny house in Scotland and was busy running a truck stop café, with her boyfriend. Chloe Marshall loved her daughters and grandchild dearly, but she didn't encourage long visits from her family—a few days were all she could tolerate!

Dr Vernon looked down at his clipboard and cleared his throat. 'Right—let's get started shall we? Staff Nurse—would you go with Dr Sinclair and look at the little boy in the paediatric department, number one cubicle? He's got a gash on his leg, and a worrying bump on the head—I don't know how he acquired it. You'd better book an X-ray.'

Tilly Rodman, passed by, pushing a dripstand, and whispered to Jandy, 'Lucky you…send Dr Sinclair along to the plaster room when you've finished with him!'

For heaven's sake, Jandy thought impatiently, the man was going to be intolerable if he felt that all the women in the unit were falling for him. She just hoped that he was good at his job.

They both walked quickly to the small wing off the main A and E department that had been designated for children. It was a small area that had been used in the past for high-dependency patients and although the walls had been decorated with nursery-rhyme characters to try and make it more child-friendly, it badly needed a make-over— and much more space.

Patrick Sinclair looked round it assessingly. 'This is the paediatric section?' he remarked with slight incredulity. 'Is there a play area here for children that are waiting to be seen?'

'We're in line to have a larger wing very soon,' said Jandy defensively. 'It's better than it used to be in the main department—of course, I'm sure you're used to state-of-the-art facilities, but we're short of cash here.'

He looked at her shrewdly as if he realised she was annoyed. 'I'm not making comparisons—Cuthbert's was a newly built hospital, so it wouldn't be fair to do so. I was merely making an observation,' he said smoothly. 'Right—shall we get started?'

Annoyed by what she took to be rather high-handed criticism of her beloved Delford Infirmary, Jandy followed him into the cubicle.

Her heart went out to the little boy—large frightened eyes looked at them owlishly through wire-rimmed glasses on a pale little face, and there were tear stains on his round cheeks. When they came in he knuckled his hand into his eyes to try and stop crying. She knew it wasn't only the pain that upset him—it was the alien surroundings and not knowing what was going to happen to him next. Despite the efforts to make the room more child-friendly to a five-year-old, the place was deeply intimidating.

A purpling bump like a dark egg was on one of the child's temples and one small leg had a long deep gash down the calf. There was something pathetic about that little limb laid across the bed.

A woman sat in a corner, looking at a magazine and chewing gum but not doing much to comfort the little boy—in fact, not taking any notice of him at all. She looked up at Patrick and Jandy with little interest, giving them a nod, and went back to her magazine.

Patrick said, 'Good morning,' to her courteously, then sat down on a chair by the bed and leaned forward to the child, trying to get his attention and distract him from his present terror. He smiled cheerfully and patted one plump little hand comfortingly.

'Hello—you're Jimmy Tate, aren't you?' he asked gently, having a swift look at the file he'd been given. 'I'm Dr Sinclair and this is Nurse Marshall, and we're going to be looking after you. Don't you worry, we'll have you feeling better in no time, Jimmy.'

Patrick's voice was soothing and the familiar clichés re-assuring. Gradually Jimmy's sobs became intermittent, just the odd one shaking his little body, and although his lip still trembled, now he was looking at Patrick, gradually relaxing a little.

Jandy swivelled the overhead light above the child so that his wounds could be seen more clearly, and reflected almost with surprise that the new registrar seemed to have a good manner with his small patient—getting Jimmy to relax and trust him went a long way towards recovery. If Dr Sinclair was arrogant, he was hiding it at the moment and she relented.

'You're a brave boy,' Patrick said, looking closely at the bruise on the child's temple and then the cut on his leg. He looked up at Jandy. 'I think we can use steri-strips for this, don't you?'

Jandy nodded and smiled reassuringly at the little boy. 'It really will feel better when I've put the magic strips on,' she said. She went to a cupboard which, when opened, revealed a stock of toys from which she pulled out a kaleidoscope. 'Have you seen one of these, Jimmy? While I'm bandaging your poorly leg, I want you to shake that and look down it—you'll see some lovely patterns there.'

Slowly Jimmy reached for the toy and put his eye to it. Jandy watched as the little boy became absorbed in what he was seeing then she started to swab the wound gently with saline solution.

Patrick turned to the woman, who'd barely looked up as they'd come in, continuing to be engrossed in her magazine. She seemed totally uninterested in what was happening to Jimmy.

'Excuse me.' His voice was courteous but firm—meant to be heeded. 'Can you tell me what happened?'

The woman stopped chewing her gum for a second and brushed a lock of greasy hair from her eyes. She had the unkempt look of someone who had lost interest in life and herself, reflected Jandy. There were a lot like her who came to Casualty.

'He fell off his bicycle and hit his head on the steps,' she said tersely. 'I told him not to ride it in the back garden with the dogs around.'

'I take it you're Mrs Tate—his mother?' asked Patrick, making a few notes.

'I'm not his mother—I'm his stepmother.'

Her voice was almost aggressive and Jandy saw Patrick look up quickly, something unfathomable in his expression, then he said smoothly, 'Has he been sick?'

'Yes—all over the floor of course.'

'I see. And did the dogs snap at him while he was riding his bike?'

Mrs Tate shrugged and said in a defensive tone, 'No, they just jumped up at him, having a bit of a lark. It was Jimmy's fault—he was teasing them. They wouldn't hurt a fly if they hadn't been provoked...he's been told often enough.' She shifted restlessly in her chair. 'Will this take long? I've got a baby at home and I had to ask my neighbour to look after her while I brought this one in.'

Patrick's eyes met Jandy's for a brief second—they were flinty hard. They were all taught to be impartial but she didn't blame him for showing a hint of the fury he

must be feeling on the child's behalf. How could anyone
be so unsympathetic to an injured five-year-old? A muscle
tightened slightly by Patrick's mouth and his voice was
clipped.

'It will take as long as it takes to see to this wound and
make sure Jimmy's not injured his skull—he'll be taken to
X-Ray in a minute. Now, can you tell me what time he had
this accident?'

'About an hour ago,' Mrs Tate replied sulkily.

'Did you see it happen?'

Her eyes shifted momentarily and she muttered, 'No—
but I sent for the ambulance as soon as I saw it was serious,'
she added self-righteously.

'Were you out when it happened?'

Again her eyes looked away from his. 'Just at a neighbour's—not far away.'

'So you don't know if the dogs attacked him?'

Jandy could almost feel Patrick Sinclair restraining himself—it wasn't their role to be judgemental, but it could be
difficult at times. He made some notes on the file and the
woman scowled.

'I told you—they wouldn't do that. Can I go now? You
can ring me when you've seen to him. Stop whinging,
Jimmy—you're a big boy now.'

Big tears had started to roll down Jimmy's cheeks again
and Jandy compressed her lips—it wasn't fair that the little
boy should be chastised.

'Perhaps you could wait and see the result of the X-ray?'
she suggested. 'It won't take me long to dress his wound.
I take it he's had his tetanus jab?'

Mrs Tate sighed heavily. 'He's had all them jabs. I'll

have to go and ring my neighbour, then...I'll be outside the entrance if you need me.'

She disappeared down towards the waiting room and Patrick turned to Jandy. 'We'll need to run blood tests, Hb, CRP and respiration checks before we take him down to X-Ray and ring up Paediatrics and get someone to look at the plates.'

Jimmy looked at them both, eyes round and anxious behind his glasses. Patrick smiled kindly at him.

'Hang on there, Jimmy, and we'll take you down to have a photograph taken of your head—it won't hurt a bit. I tell you what, Nurse Marshall, I think this little boy's been one of the bravest we've had here today—I think he deserves something special!'

His blue eyes looked at her questioningly—not having worked at this hospital before, he wouldn't know what rewards they offered their little patients.

Jandy grinned. 'Quite right, Doctor—I've got a special medal for someone like Jimmy!'

She opened a drawer and handed Patrick a plastic medal with 'Very Brave Patient' printed on it, which Patrick pinned on Jimmy's jumper. The little boy stared down at it then looked up at the adults with a shy smile.

'Is it mine?' he asked. It was the first time he'd spoken.

'It certainly is—you deserve it, sweetheart,' said Jandy. 'And now we'll take you to have that photograph taken.'

'I'm not happy with that head wound and the fact he's been sick,' said Patrick as he and Jandy walked back from the paediatric section, leaving Tilly Rodman to stay with Jimmy and read him a story. 'Have you rung Paediatrics yet? He'll be kept in anyway for observation, whatever the results are.'

Jandy nodded. 'They've got a bed—and at least it gives him a night away from that ghastly woman. She'd obviously left him alone while she gossiped with her friend.'

Patrick's expression darkened, and Jandy noticed the small scar at the side of his face seemed more pronounced and livid.

'I can't tell you how angry that woman makes me,' he said in a controlled, terse tone that only emphasised his disgust. 'I've no doubt that that little boy's not having a very happy life. I'll talk to the child liaison officer about my concerns regarding the stepmother—no child should be at the mercy of someone like that. I didn't see a shred of affection or compassion for Jimmy.'

There was such suppressed venom in his voice that Jandy looked at him with surprise. She would have thought he'd have taken a more measured approach—still taking it just as seriously but not quite so personally. After all, in an A and E department it wasn't unusual to come across a case like Jimmy's.

'It's really got to you, hasn't it?' she said.

He looked down at her and shrugged. 'I guess I went over the top a bit there—took it to heart. I should be more objective, I know.' He bunched his hands in his pockets. 'Sorry—it's a bit of a hobby horse of mine.'

Jandy nodded, slightly bemused by this worldly-wise doctor's soft centre—somehow she felt there was a hidden agenda behind his words.

'I feel that way too,' she said. 'I don't know how anyone could be as callous as she was…but it happens, doesn't it?

We see all sorts of cases here and often it's quite heart-rending. And, of course, if we have any doubts about Jimmy's treatment, we should have it investigated.'

Patrick looked down at her upturned concerned face with her wide brown eyes illuminated by a beam of sunshine through the window, honey-blonde hair shining in its light—some had escaped from the band that held it back, and suddenly he pictured how it would spill out like a sheet of soft gold over her shoulders if the band was pulled away completely…

He smiled wryly to himself. How long ago had it been since he'd touched a woman or had any kind of intimacy with one? Oh, sure, he'd thought about it when he'd been the odd one out at a party when everyone else had a partner, or lying awake in the early hours and feeling sorry for himself. But that one memorable disaster three years ago had ensured that he'd kept well away from anything but mild flirtations since then.

Of course, he thought sadly, once he'd had everything—a wonderful woman, a perfect life, and then like a bolt from the blue it had come to an end, and he couldn't imagine ever having it again. He clenched his fists together to control his emotions. Stop it, he told himself fiercely—don't go there! He had his darling Livy to think of now.

Then he sighed as he refocused on the real world. 'I'd better go and write up this case report,' he said abruptly, shifting his gaze from her face. 'See you soon.'

Jandy stared rather bemusedly after his tall retreating figure as he strode back to the desk. When Patrick had looked at her with those intense blue eyes of his, she had felt the oddest little tug on her heart, a flicker of attraction.

How peculiar was that, when only a few minutes before she'd been annoyed by his criticism of the paediatric department—another bighead from London who probably thought he knew everything!

She went to clear up the cubicle that Jimmy had occupied and reflected crossly that she hadn't thought for a long time about men, except for the need to steer clear of them as much as possible. Then a man walked into the department with an attractive smile and amazing blue eyes and suddenly she was imagining all kinds of things! She shook her head irritably. Being too aware of married men and their thoughts was a dangerous pastime—they were strictly off-limits to her. What she had to concentrate on was finding a new place for her, Abigail and Lydia to live—and soon!

CHAPTER TWO

AFTER the initial flurry of cases there was a lull. Typical of A and E—one couldn't predict what was going to come in, although generally Friday and Saturday nights were mayhem. Jandy finished checking the cubicles for supplies of bandages, paper towels and latex gloves, and during the ten minutes allotted for her lunch decided to ring her sister and ask her to get in touch with the agent about the lease of the house. There was no possibility of buying it, but perhaps the owner could be persuaded to give them a little more time to find something else.

Jandy walked quickly down the corridor to the pay-phone in Reception as Delford A and E was firmly against the use of mobile phones in the department. It was typical that someone was already using the phone, she thought with irritation. She leant against the wall near the kiosk, hoping the man would see she was waiting, then she realised that it was Patrick Sinclair.

Watching him now, she wondered what had made her think there had been anything remotely intimate in the way he had looked at her earlier. He was just an ordinary guy who happened to have the kind of sexy looks that would draw some women's eyes—over six feet of impressive body, in fact, and thick dark hair, endearingly rumpled—but he wasn't all that special, was he?

He finished his conversation, came out of the kiosk and gave her a smile and a half-wave as he passed her—she was surprised at the little frisson of excitement she felt when he did that. She found herself smiling as she dialled her sister's mobile number and started to speak to her.

'Hi, Lydia—did you get onto the agent about the house? I left the letter on the kitchen table…'

Karen Borley was writing up the whiteboard when Jandy returned. She looked at Jandy's exasperated face.

'Has something happened?' she enquired.

Jandy groaned. 'I've just been speaking to my sister. She's been in touch with the agent and we definitely have to be out in four weeks—sooner if possible! Can you believe Lydia has told the agent we'd be interested in a massive house at an enormous monthly rent? She seems to think we're rolling in money.'

'Oh, dear—Lydia is rather impetuous, isn't she?' said Karen vaguely as she shuffled through some case sheets.

'Of course she's away the next week,' added Jandy, 'Leaving me to organise everything! Typical!'

Patrick Sinclair looked up from the computer and said noncommittally, 'If you really are stuck for somewhere to live, I do happen to know a place that's empty and needs a tenant—it's a bit neglected and it's in the country, so it may not suit you. But if you get desperate…'

Jandy was surprised that a man like him should bother himself with her problems. 'Really? It's very kind of you to suggest it… I might be very interested…do you know the owner?'

He nodded. 'Yes—I know him well.'

'Perhaps if you could find out the rent he's asking…'

'No problem,' Patrick started to say, when Karen put down the phone and interrupted them, her cheeks slightly pink as if she'd heard something of interest. She looked around, making sure no one was listening.

'Mr Vernon's just been on to me about a patient he's been looking at in the small theatre,' she said in a hushed voice. 'He was picked up by the police outside a pub earlier this morning and taken back to the station on a drunk and disorderly charge. Evidently he'd had a bit of a fracas with some young lads…but it's rather a delicate situation.'

'So far normal,' murmured Jandy. 'So why is it a delicate situation?'

Sister flicked a look at her and said impressively, 'I think you'll know what I mean when you see him—it's Leo Parker, the agony uncle who does that chat show on television.'

Jandy raised her eyebrows. 'Wow! Leo Parker, the Voice of Reason? The press will be interested, won't they?'

'Exactly!' Karen pursed her lips. 'I don't want a word of who this patient is to get out—I can't bear those journalists running all over the place, disrupting the department, questioning everybody. If they get a whiff of this, it'll be bedlam.'

'Better prepare for bedlam, then,' Jandy said under her breath. 'This place is like a sieve when it comes to gossip!'

She heard Patrick chuckle as they filed into the cubicle. 'Sounds familiar…' he murmured.

'Mr Parker was just about conscious when he was brought in,' explained Karen. 'The police were concerned that it might not be just drink that's affecting him and that he could have had a crack on the head.'

'Are his X-rays clear?' asked Patrick.

'Not a sign of anything. Mr Vernon has already had a look at his skull plates—quite normal. But he's in and out of consciousness, so something's wrong. We're waiting for his bloods to come back, but I'd like him closely monitored. Give me a shout if you find anything.'

Leo Parker lay on the bed, the impressive head of thick grey hair, which was his trademark, matted with blood from a gash on his forehead. He shifted restlessly from side to side, moving his limbs and muttering incoherently. Jandy was struck by how ordinary he looked, just as vulnerable as every other patient who came in to A and E reduced to helplessness by their condition.

'Poor man—not quite the towering TV personality at the moment,' murmured Jandy, looking at the trace on the graph over the bed giving his oxygen levels and pulse rate. 'Heart rate's accelerated and his BP's quite low.'

'He's right out of it at the moment,' commented Patrick, bending over the man and shining a small torch into the pupil of each eye. Then he bent the patient's legs, striking below the knees sharply. 'His reflexes seem OK. What about his plantar reflex?'

Jandy took a pencil out of her pocket and drew it across the base of the man's foot, which curled in response.

'Nothing wrong there...' She bent forward and sniffed the man's breath. 'Nice and beery—he's obviously had a few bevies,' she remarked. She frowned and sniffed again. 'Wait a minute...there's something else... Funny smell... acetone, I think.'

Patrick leaned close to the man and nodded back at her, touching the man's face. 'Absolutely right—he's sweaty as well. Alcohol-induced hypoglycaemia,' he added almost to himself. 'I don't suppose he checked his blood-sugar levels after having a bit to drink. That's why his speech is so garbled—his glucose levels will be very low.'

'If he'd been left in that police cell, it could have been curtains.'

'Yup—he's lucky they brought him in when they did. We'll give him fifty grams of glucose intravenously. I take it the packs are in the cupboard up there?'

Jandy handed Patrick one of the pre-packed syringes and they both watched the patient after he'd been injected to see how long it took for him to come round.

'If only he realised the harm he could do to himself when he drinks,' he remarked drily. 'Because he's diabetic everything can shut down when the nervous system becomes sluggish…organ damage, brain damage, you name it.'

Leo gradually opened his eyes and looked around him in a confused way. 'Hello, there,' Patrick said. 'Feeling a bit better, Mr Parker? I think you're nearly with us again.'

The man gazed up at him blankly, blinking his eyes and staring around fuzzily, his system trying to restore reactions and memory.

'Well, that took just over a minute—miraculous!' murmured Patrick. He nodded at Jandy approvingly.

God, his eyes were amazing! Once again they seemed to hold hers for a second before she could drag her glance away. Irritably she thought that it was becoming something of a habit, imagining that the man was looking at her in some sort of special way. He wasn't hers to fantasise about.

She reached into the cupboard without comment and slipped on latex gloves before starting to swab the cut on Leo Parker's head. He made a feeble attempt to bat her hand away then began to stir, trying to sit up before flopping back against the pillow.

'Where am I?' he mumbled.

'You're in Delford General Casualty Department,' said Patrick. 'You overdid the alcohol, I'm afraid…not a good idea when you're diabetic. We'll get you a bed.'

There was a sudden pause, and a girl's impatient voice floated over to them beyond the curtain. 'I need to see Leo now. I was with him when he fell…he'll want me with him…'

'Are you a relative?' Jandy recognised the voice of Danny Smith, the A and E receptionist.

'I'm his partner—and his PA.' The girl's voice sounded defiant. 'Delphine Hunt.'

'Well, the doctor's looking at him now—can you wait a minute?'

Patrick went over to the curtains and swished them back. 'You can come in now if you like—Mr Parker's coming round gradually. Perhaps you can tell us what happened.'

Delphine Hunt had bright red hair cascading past her shoulders, and a very short dress under a fake-fur evening jacket. She brushed Patrick aside without a word and flung herself onto the bed next to Leo Parker, kissing him passionately then breaking into sobs. 'Babe—are you OK? I've been out of my mind with worry…'

'Hey—wait a moment,' said Patrick, moving forward and pulling the girl away. 'Let the patient breathe! He's just coming out of a diabetic coma—he's not fit to be manhandled.'

'Is he going to be OK? I thought those thugs were going to kill him…' Delphine started to cry and the make-up around her eyes ran in little black rivulets down her cheeks.

Jandy pushed a chair forward. 'Why don't you sit down here and tell us what happened?' she said gently.

'And keep your voice down please,' added Patrick drily.

'We…we were having a quiet drink, and these yobbos started calling him names, just because he's on TV.' Delphine pulled a handkerchief out of her pocket and blew her nose. 'Leo's a bit impetuous and he went over and had it out with them…and the next thing he's on the floor and the police have been called. They said he was drunk and disorderly. He never was—he'd only had a few, and it wasn't his fault at all!'

'I guess you've been trying to get to him since he was taken to the police station, haven't you?' said Patrick.

'I'd just got to the station when the ambulance drove off and I saw Leo being taken on it and driven away…they wouldn't tell me a thing.'

From the bed, Leo Parker whispered, 'Delphine—what are you doing here?'

The girl took his hands. 'Oh, babe, you're OK. Thank God!' She turned to Patrick and Jandy. 'Can we go now? I'll call a taxi.'

'Mr Parker certainly can't go,' interrupted Patrick sternly. 'You need to stay in overnight—we've got to get you balanced,' he said to Leo. 'You know that, don't you, or you might find yourself in a coma again.'

Leo struggled to sit up. 'I can't stay here the night,' he said, aghast. 'I've got to be at the studio by lunchtime. What time is it now?'

'Ten-thirty—you won't have time to recover properly by then,' said Jandy.

'I will,' said Leo, his voice slurring slightly. He swung his legs over the bed and started to get down. 'I'm going to discharge myself—I'm perfectly all right.'

Patrick put his hand on the man's shoulder. 'You've got to give yourself time to recover—drink and diabetes don't mix. And you've got a nasty gash on your head.'

Leo stared at them all and then, as if the reality of the situation fully hit him, put a hand over his face and groaned.

'Oh, my God. If the press get hold of this…' He looked up at them pleadingly. 'If this gets into the papers, I'm sunk. I'm recording a show about alcohol abuse today. I can't let it get out that I've had a bit too much of the sauce myself.'

'Everything here is strictly confidential,' Patrick promised.

Leo looked at him wryly. 'Things have a funny way of getting out into the public domain, you know.'

'Then let's go now, Leo, darling, before anyone knows. I've booked us into the hotel together,' said Delphine eagerly, laying a possessive hand on his arm.

Leo sighed heavily. 'Have you got two rooms?'

Delphine looked a little abashed. 'Well—no. You said we could be together, babe…'

'You silly mare! Do you think the press are dumb? My PA and I sharing a room doesn't look good—have you forgotten I'm a family man to the public?'

Jandy flicked the briefest of glances towards Patrick over Delphine's head, and his gaze held hers for a fraction of a second, before returning impassively to the scene before him.

'I really wouldn't advise you leaving the hospital yet,' he said firmly.

'Advise what you like—but don't ruin my career. I'll do what I damn well like. I can discharge myself if I want to.'

He was interrupted in mid-sentence by the sound of the curtains being viciously flung back, and a small plump woman stood before them, staring at Leo Parker with undisguised fury.

'So you've done it again, have yóu?' she said coldly. 'Will you never learn, you old fool? And you can forget about discharging yourself as well.'

There was a short silence then Patrick said evenly, 'Excuse me, but just who are you?'

The woman turned to him and said icily, 'I'm Phyllis Parker, young man, Leo Parker's wife, and I'm just about sick of him making such a Charlie of himself!'

'Oh, God—Phyllis!' Leo Parker flopped back on his pillows and closed his eyes. In the corner, Delphine began to cry.

Patrick and Jandy watched as Leo Parker was pushed down the corridor on the way to Medical, closely followed by his wife, still berating him. They disappeared into the lift and Patrick and Jandy went into Sister Borley's office behind the central station.

He turned to Jandy and said sardonically, 'I've never watched his programme before, but I'm going to make a point of seeing it and hearing his views on family life and the evils of drink.'

'Same here,' said Jandy, trying to keep a straight face.

'I reckon Leo Parker's going to have some explaining to do...'

His clear blue eyes laughed down at her, his grave face

softened by humour, and Jandy answered his amusement with a grin, mutually diverted by the little scene that had just played out. Patrick Sinclair could be quite engaging when he wanted to, she admitted.

Karen put down the phone she'd been speaking into. 'That,' she said with compressed lips, 'was the *Delford Gazette*. It's already got out that Leo Parker's a patient here—and I'm not surprised after all the fuss!'

She went out of the room and wiped the whiteboard vigorously, venting her irritation by obliterating the annoying Mr Parker's name now he had been taken to the medical ward. Jandy went to deal with a young girl with a staple stuck down her fingernail.

It was a fairly routine afternoon—a sprained ankle, a scalded arm and a child with a hacking cough who should have been taken to see his G.P., according to Mr Vernon, and not brought to A and E, cluttering up the department.

Karen sat down at her desk with a sigh of relief. 'Right,' she said comfortably. 'At last! Time for a breather. It could be a chance for us to catch up on all the patient assessment forms and maybe—'

The sudden jarring sound of the trauma bleep split the air. 'Trauma call, trauma call, trauma team to A and E Resus. ETA three minutes...trauma call...'

Karen swore softly to herself. 'Wouldn't you know it? I spoke too soon.'

The relaxed atmosphere changed and there was an air of tension as everyone available gathered round the central station, prepared to spring into action.

Tim Vernon came out of a cubicle, swinging his stethoscope impatiently as if he couldn't wait to get going, and

Max Fuller, the porter, started pushing trolleys down the passage and out of the way of the entrance. Karen's voice was authoritative and clipped, her look of motherly cosiness changed to brisk efficiency as she spoke on the phone to the ambulancemen.

'OK, everyone—an RTA on the main Delford road. My information is that there's an injured female hit by a motorcycle, lacerations to her face and in great pain. A cyclist with obvious fracture of right leg, and a pillion passenger with a very low BP and head injury, possible status 3. ETA any minute now.' She put down the phone and turned to the staff. 'Patrick, you take the injured female with lacerations on her face in Theatre One and the status 3 patient will go into the big theatre.'

'I'll take the status 3 patient,' said Dr Vernon. 'Bob— you come with me.'

'That's three patients for urgent X-rays. John Cooper can take the suspect broken leg with Tilly. Max—make sure we've got enough oxygen cylinders and dripstands in that big theatre. Jandy, can you be on hand to help where necessary?'

Jandy felt the familiar ripple of adrenalin kicking through her body as they waited for the ambulances to arrive. It was peculiar to Casualty—that tremor of excitement mixed with apprehension in dealing with absolutely any injury or illness thrown at them, and often time was not on their side. Split-second decisions had to be made and the staff in the department were the first line of defence.

Tilly nibbled at her nails nervously. 'It's nerve-racking, not knowing what you'll get. I hate these horrible accidents. I'm frightened I'll faint or something.'

Jandy placed a reassuring hand on Tilly's arm—the young nurse had only been in the department a few weeks and it was a very fast learning curve for all the students.

'It's always a bit scary—knowing that how we deal with patients here can determine the outcome of their eventual recovery. And every case is different,' she admitted. 'But once we're in the thick of it, there's no time to think. You put everything else out of your head.'

Patrick stood near the door, looking down the drive where the ambulances would come from. He turned and smiled at the young nurse. 'But this is what it's all about, isn't it? Being able to turn your hand to anything. In the end it becomes instinctive. It's exciting!'

He grinned at Jandy, eyes dancing with anticipation, confidently looking forward to the challenge of the un-known. Everyone's idea of the perfect doctor, she thought wryly, his hospital greens seeming to emphasise his athletic physique. She was uneasily aware that she was just a little too conscious of Patrick's attraction and that devastating easy smile of his, but he was just an ordinary married guy, wasn't he? Not her type at all. She bit her lip. This man was getting too much under her skin.

She glanced at Bob Thoms—what a contrast! His brow was furrowed with anxiety as usual. He was a good doctor, painstaking and thorough, but always racked by worries that his best might not be good enough—what a pity she couldn't find someone like him attractive. Bob was free and single with no hint of arrogance or over-confidence about him—but incredibly dull!

She forced herself to concentrate on the moment, to push out of her mind the distracting fact that Patrick was standing close to her. Then the flashing blue lights of the ambulances appeared as they came up the drive, and gradually the whine of the sirens died down as they reached the entrance. In a few minutes the doors swished open and three trolleys were being pushed through into the wide passage. A plump woman clutching a large handbag was running beside one of the trolleys, tears streaming down her face. Jandy took her arm gently but firmly and steered her to the side of the passage.

'Come with me for a minute,' she said gently. 'Just let the doctors see to the patient… Are you a relative?'

'I'm her mother…Mrs Thorpe…' The woman clung to Jandy hysterically, hiccuping sobs shaking her, as the shock of the incident she'd just witnessed set in. 'She…she's having a baby. Please help her. She mustn't lose this one—she's had two miscarriages already.'

'Come with me to the desk and let's take her details. First, what's her name?'

'Brenda Evans…she's twenty-five. She's been longing for this baby…'

Mrs Thorpe's voice started to rise in panic again and Jandy quickly said, 'Tell me what happened…take it slowly.'

Gradually the woman started to calm down, and in the telling of the story her mind was forced to concentrate on something other than what was now happening to her daughter.

'This motorbike…it came towards us with no warning. It was going that fast. I saw it coming, and I screamed to Brenda, but it hit her and sent her sprawling on the ground.' Mrs Thorpe paused for a second to control her tears. 'Will…will she lose the baby?'

With the skill born of much practice in calming worried relatives, Jandy led her to a chair and said comfortingly, 'She's in very good hands, Mrs Thorpe, and I know they will be monitoring her very closely—especially now they know her medical history. I'm going to get you a cup of tea and then I'll go and find out just what's happening to her. You try and calm down—she'll need you to look after her when she goes home.'

A paramedic was wheeling Mrs Thorpe's daughter briskly into one of the small theatres. 'This is Brenda Evans,' he said. 'She's in a lot of pain, but superficially at least she only seems to have lacerations. BP 100 over 70 , pulse 120. Reasonably stable. She's also seven and a half months pregnant.'

'What happened?' asked Patrick, bending over the supine figure on the trolley.

'It looks like a motorcycle tried to take a corner at speed and hit this lady a glancing blow—she fell forward onto her face.'

Jandy had come into the cubicle to see what was happening so that she could update the patient's mother on the latest information. She was watching the girl's face—there was a large graze on her chin, covered with grit.

'She's very pale...' she murmured to Patrick. 'Obviously she's in shock, but she's blinking her eyes all the time. What's causing that?'

He frowned and looked at Brenda's face closely. 'Rapid blinking is often a sign of a sharp pain. I wonder... Can you speak, Brenda?'

Brenda grimaced and mumbled something through stiff lips.

'I reckon it's something to do with her jaw—see how

stiffly she's holding it,' Patrick said. 'Moving it seems to cause her extreme discomfort.'

He ran his hands lightly over her face, watching her reactions carefully. Brenda sucked in her breath and groaned.

'I'm sorry, Brenda,' he said gently. 'That's all I'm going to do at the moment. We'll give you something for the pain, don't worry. You'll be all right—just try and relax and don't do anything that might move your jaw.'

He patted her arm, trying to reassure her and with his calm voice showing her that he was very much in charge. You got to know people's skills quite quickly when you worked with them in Casualty, reflected Jandy. Patrick had a sure touch with patients, knowing that the familiar platitudes would soothe Brenda. He knew that physical and aural contact with a frightened patient could reduce the effects of shock.

It was one of Karen's repeated adages to her team: 'Remember that reassurance is one of the most powerful clinical tools you've got.' When it came to medicine, Dr Sinclair was ticking quite a few boxes so far, admitted Jandy.

'Can you arrange to have Brenda X-rayed ASAP?' Patrick asked Jandy.

'But she's pregnant,' she pointed out.

Patrick shook his head. 'She's going to need surgery on her jaw, I'm afraid, and we've got to know exactly what the damage is. The X-ray won't be over the baby—fortunately she's late on in her pregnancy.'

'Do you think she's broken her jaw?'

'The first thing to hit the floor was her chin I reckon—like that!' Patrick demonstrated this by smacking his fist into his other hand. 'That's where the cut is. I'll bet what's happened is that the force of the impact has snapped off her left condyle—the part of the bone that forms the hinge of the jaw.'

'She hit her chin just at the wrong point, then.'

Patrick nodded. 'Every time she moves her jaw, bone fragments are scraping across the tissue surrounding her ear.'

Jandy grimaced. 'Poor woman—that's seriously painful. What about pain relief?'

'After her X-ray give her ten milligrams of morphine and get her booked into Surgical—I'll speak to the surgical registrar. We need someone from Maternity to look her over as well. We don't want her having this baby yet.'

Jandy split open a pair of lanolin gloves and with exquisite gentleness swabbed the wound on Brenda's chin. 'Her mother's really anxious about her,' she said. 'I think it would help if you explained Brenda's injuries rather than me—you're the expert.'

He laughed. 'I'll do my best.'

Patrick sat down next to Mrs Thorpe on one of the chairs in the corridor, leaning towards her as he described what he thought had happened, giving a short but lucid explanation. Gradually the tension left the woman's face until she was actually giving a watery smile by the time he was called away to the phone.

'Oh, he's a lovely man that Dr Sinclair,' said Mrs Thorpe when Jandy returned from trying to get a slot for Brenda's X-ray. 'I feel she's in really good hands. Could I go and see Brenda now?'

Jandy smiled. 'I'm sure it would do her good if you just sat by her and held her hand until they take her for X-rays. The calmer she's kept, the better.'

'I understand,' said Mrs Thorpe. The tea and the chat to

Patrick about her daughter had composed her and she was ready to cope again. She followed Jandy to the small theatre where her daughter was and sat by her bed, flicking a wondering eye at all the monitoring equipment around the bed.

'Eh, it's like a space capsule in here,' she said. 'I've never seen so many tubes and dials!'

She picked up her daughter's hand and squeezed it. 'You'll be alright, love,' she said softly. 'I've had a chat to that Dr Sinclair—he's doing his best for you, I know.'

Patrick popped his head round the curtain. 'Has the X-ray been booked yet?' he asked.

'There's a bit of a delay—one of the machines is being serviced and there's a queue for the other,' Jandy informed him.

He frowned. 'For God's sake—surely it's usual to service the machines at a quieter time? How long are they going to be?'

'About twenty minutes, I think.'

'That's ridiculous! This needs to be done immediately—surely there should be a procedure for urgent cases?'

Jandy sympathised with him. It was incredibly frustrating to have treatment blocked for the patient, but she also noticed the implied criticism of the hospital. Poor old Delford General wasn't awash with funds for any more X-ray machines.

'I'm sorry, there's not much I can do about it. There's only one machine at the moment for a lot of patients.'

'I'm not accusing you of causing the hold-up,' he said tersely. Then his tone softened. 'I'm sorry—I'm not knocking Delford, believe me.'

He looked at her steadily then left the room, and she blushed at his accurate reading of her thoughts. Actually, she agreed with him that somewhere along the line there had been inefficiency. Perhaps she was being a little too prickly where Patrick was concerned!

Karen bustled up to Jandy, her pale blue tunic top straining slightly over her full figure, her face pink from exertion. Jandy often wondered why Karen was so plump as she seemed to run everywhere, and had an inexhaustible supply of energy.

'Ah, there you are,' she puffed. 'I think we're under control now. Dr Vernon's booked the head injury into the neurological ward for obs, and Brenda Evans will be prepped for Theatre later.' She shot a look at her watch. 'Time for the handover soon and then home, sweet home, thank goodness!' Her voice dropped. 'By the way, I'm rather impressed by Patrick Sinclair—aren't you? As I said before, he seems extremely capable!'

'Yes,' allowed Jandy cautiously.

He seemed extremely everything—wonderful with his patients and a good clinician. But she still had reservations about this self-assured man and his drop-dead handsome looks—she would see how he performed over the next few weeks! Men like him tended to be arrogant, everything dropping into their laps very easily, and she could see how he might break some poor girl's heart if he was free. What a good job it was that he was a family man and a no-go area—she'd learned from her own experience that loving a married man was not an option.

CHAPTER THREE

'I DON'T believe this,' muttered Jandy, looking at the huge tailback of vehicles round the car park. For the third time that month the car-park barrier had jammed and from her experience it could take at least three quarters of an hour to sort out. Nothing for it but to get the bus and leave the car in the car park—she hated to keep Pippa waiting when she was due to pick up Abigail. It had been a gruelling week and she was tired—although her fears about working with the new registrar had been groundless.

After two weeks she was beginning to realise that Patrick Sinclair was not only a good doctor but surprisingly easy to work with. She didn't know much about his family—he never talked much about his life outside the hospital, but he could be a laugh. In fact, she admitted as she trudged to the bus stop, she actually looked forward to coming to work with him. Once she'd even caught herself wishing that he'd been unattached, fantasising about how different her attitude toward him might have been if he was single—but, then, of course, there would have been a deluge of women waiting to snap him up!

It started to rain as she waited hopefully by the bus stop,

then a car drew up in front of her and the passenger window was lowered.

'Can I give you a lift?' said a familiar voice. 'It's getting very wet.'

Jandy bent down to see who it was and found herself looking into the blue eyes of the very man she'd been thinking of! Patrick was right—the rain seemed to be getting harder all the time and she could feel rivulets of water making their way down her back. It was ridiculous how her heart started thumping at his invitation—it was only a lift in his car, for heaven's sake, not an indecent proposal!

'Are you sure?' she asked. 'I'd be really grateful, but I may be taking you miles out of your way.'

'No problem,' he said. 'Jump in.'

Jandy relaxed back in the blessed warmth of the car, and glanced across at Patrick, his strong profile outlined in the dark as he looked in the rear-view mirror before pulling out into the road. Inside the car it felt intimate, cosy. Her eyes fastened on his hands on the steering-wheel, strong, capable hands, and she felt the flutter of excitement she used to feel when she went on a date with someone she liked, anticipating the evening to come. Stop this, she said fiercely to herself. Her reaction to him was becoming almost like the reflex action of a tap on the knee joint. He was a married man she'd only known for two weeks, for heaven's sake.

'This is good of you,' she murmured. 'I would've been very late picking Abigail up from the childminder. The barriers in the car park are always getting stuck—it's the second time I've had to leave the car there all night.'

'A damn nuisance for you. How old is your little girl?'

'She's four—Pippa takes her to and from nursery school, which is wonderful. How about your daughter—what age is she?'

He smiled. 'The same age as your Abigail. Her name's Livy—short for Olivia—and she's at nursery school as well. I'll be picking her up from the after-school club they have there.'

They had stopped at traffic lights and the glow from a streetlamp fell on a photograph pinned to the dashboard. It showed a curly-headed child in the arms of an attractive, laughing woman. Jandy bent forward to look at it more closely. This must be his wife and daughter. What a lovely family he had—and what a wonderful father he would be, she thought wistfully. That was something Abigail would never know—a father's love and attention, a man she could always trust throughout her life.

She smothered a sigh and said brightly, 'And this is a photo of Livy and your wife, I suppose—they're very beautiful.'

Patrick nodded and said briefly, 'Yes—it's a good photograph.'

'And is your wife medical?' asked Jandy, assuming that she worked as Patrick had to pick his daughter up.

Patrick was silent for a moment and Jandy wondered if he'd heard her, then eventually he spoke, his voice quiet but brutally harsh. 'My wife died three and a half years ago—she had an accident. Livy doesn't remember her mother at all.'

For a second the bald statement hung in the air, horrifying, unbelievable. Patrick looked across at Jandy as she caught her breath in distress.

'I'm sorry,' he said more gently. 'I always have difficulty telling people that—but there's no easy way to say it.'

What an idiot I am, thought Jandy wretchedly. 'I…I'm so sorry, Patrick. I didn't mean to pry. I just assumed…'

'It's not your fault,' he said tersely. 'You weren't to know that Rachel had died…but it's tough being on your own.'

There was a weary sadness in his face—Jandy guessed every time he told this story it was like knives going through him. She was silent for a few minutes, contemplating the tragedy that had happened to him—his beautiful young wife killed before her baby grew up and bringing a happy marriage to an abrupt end. He had obviously loved Rachel very much, whereas her love for Terry had long disappeared. Now she only felt contempt for the man who had treated her so badly.

'Being a single parent isn't easy,' she said softly. 'I know, because I'm a single parent as well.'

He flicked a surprised look at her. 'That's terrible. I'm so sorry to hear that. When were you widowed?' he asked.

It was so stupid. She was over Terry now, long over him, and yet she still felt treacherous tears welling up in her eyes whenever someone was sympathetic—especially someone like Patrick who'd gone through traumas of his own. Just when she thought she had her emotions under control, something would trigger the sadness of loneliness and rejection. And it wasn't the thought that Terry had never loved her that upset her now—just the legacy of emotions he'd left her and how he'd changed the person she had once been.

If she started telling her life story now, she would probably start blubbing properly. And perhaps it would almost sound as if she was trying to compete in the bad-luck stakes if she revealed everything.

'I…I wasn't widowed—that's not why I'm single. I'll tell you another time about it,' she said quickly, swallowing hard to get rid of the lump of self-pity that had lodged in her throat. 'But it's a long boring story.' With relief she saw that they had arrived at Pippa's. 'Ah, here we are. You can drop me off at the gate.'

'I can take you both home if you like.'

'No, really, we'll be fine. It's stopped raining and we literally live round the corner. Thank you very much—I'm so grateful.'

She had started to gabble a little and suddenly she wanted to be out of the car. She'd intruded on private grief and felt embarrassed that she'd become emotional herself.

'I'll see you tomorrow, then.' She pulled the handle of the door to get out. It didn't move as she tugged it. 'Oh…I think it's locked,' she said.

'Damn—I've had a little trouble with it—the central locking system's a bit dodgy.' Patrick leant across her and punched a button on the side of the door.

He was very, very close to her—she felt his breath on her cheek, she could smell his warmth, the remnants of aftershave put on that morning, see the occasional grey hair on his temples and the slightly raised skin of the scar on his face. If he leant any further forward his chest would be jammed against her body. She closed her eyes, and like a flicker of lightning she felt the dangerous flash of attraction to a very sexy man. She had a ridiculous urge to put her cheek next to his, feel his mouth on hers and lean against that broad chest. She swallowed hard, and her heart beat a little tattoo against her ribs, a kaleidoscope of emotions whirling round in her head at this sudden sizzling magnetism she felt for Patrick. But, then, it wasn't really all that sudden, was it? Over two weeks she'd been suppressing a growing awareness of Patrick's charismatic appeal.

Patrick pulled back abruptly, and took a deep breath. 'There—the door should open now,' he said slightly huskily, then he cleared his throat and murmured, 'I'm very sorry. It was tactless of me to ask if you were a widow— it's upset you.'

'Of course it hasn't.' She forced herself to sound brisk and controlled. 'I'm over it now.'

He shook his head. 'Believe me, I know what it's like to be alone.'

Their eyes clashed in a mutual response of compassion, two people who knew what it was to lose love, albeit in very different ways, each haunted by tragic memories.

Then behind them a car hooted and roared past them and the spell was broken.

There was a short silence and then Patrick remarked casually, 'Look, perhaps we could introduce our daughters to each other some time—Livy doesn't know many other children around here yet and it would be great to get together. I'm sure there's so much around here that we could all enjoy.'

Was there something in his expression that seemed to translate into 'that you and I could enjoy', or was she reading too much into it? Whatever, she felt a little thrill of pleasure that he was keen to see her again.

'That's a great idea—we must definitely do that!'

'Then we'll think of something…'

His voice trailed off and their eyes locked for a moment, until out of embarrassment Jandy said quickly, 'Right—I must go now.' She jumped out of the car and waved at him before she went up the path. 'Thanks again for the lift, Patrick,' she called.

And for the rest of the evening her emotions were in turmoil—sympathy over Patrick's terrible loss, alternating with the realisation that he had lit a spark of desire inside her that she'd thought had gone for ever. Had he felt it too? Probably not, she told herself sharply. It had probably meant no more to him than comforting a child who'd been hurt—after all, how could she compete with the memory of a beloved and beautiful wife?

'What are we having for tea, Daddy? Can we have sausages and baked beans—I like that! Did you hear me, Daddy—did you?'

Patrick looked in the rear-view mirror at Livy, chattering away behind him, and laughed.

'Yes, sweetheart—of course you can. And perhaps some ice cream afterwards?'

'Yes!' shouted Livy, rocking backwards and forwards in her car seat with delight. 'Grandpa can have some too!'

'That's a good idea, Livy. We'll be back at Easterleigh soon and you can tell him what you've been doing at nursery school.'

Livy settled back in her seat and started to suck her thumb, her eyes drooping, and Patrick reflected sadly that it was at this time of day that he felt Rachel's loss most of all. There should be a mother waiting at home to greet his little daughter, someone with better culinary skills than his basic sausages, fish fingers or mince. Someone, he sighed, who could help him with the strain of coping with a demanding father and an energetic four-year-old. Oh, there was Sheena, the housekeeper, and she was marvellous, but she was getting on, and he felt he should do as much as he could for Livy when he wasn't working.

He flicked a glance at the little girl now asleep in the back of the car. The intense grief he'd felt with Rachel's death had turned to a gentle sadness over the years, but the guilt about causing that death was still as burning as ever. If only they hadn't had a stupid row about something as trivial as shopping, after he'd told her he'd be late home that evening as he was playing squash after work.

Her voice still rang in his ears. 'You do remember we're having a supper party tonight and you said you'd get the wine?'

He'd been short with her, tired after too many tense days at work. 'For God's sake, can't you get it when you go shopping? I only get so much free time,' he'd snapped.

'I did all that yesterday,' she'd snapped back at him. 'I'll have to make a special journey now.'

And she had done, thankfully leaving Livy with her friend then driving through pelting rain down the bypass to the shops. A car had skidded coming towards her…she hadn't stood a chance. If he had picked up the wine on his way home, as he could have done so easily, she would still be alive and Livy would have a mother. If only… He would never forgive himself—never forgive himself that his last words to her had been in anger.

There'd been plenty of opportunities to get married again, had he taken them up—but he'd made a terrible mistake after Rachel had died, flinging himself into a relationship that had nearly ended in disaster. He'd learned his lesson now, he thought grimly. Never again would he reveal his background until he was absolutely sure that the woman he was dating loved him for himself alone and would love Livy almost as much as he did.

And why should he be dwelling on this now? He smiled grimly. It was because he'd met Jandy Marshall, sure that he had felt the crackle of sexual tension between them in the closeness of the car. It was as if two electric contacts had touched and a spark had been ignited. And he had been totally and utterly shaken by it.

He changed gear viciously as he went round a corner—it was just his luck that he should be drawn to a beautiful girl like her at this stage of his life. And how dangerous was that? He knew nothing about her at all except that she was single, and that she had enough on her plate without taking on another child—and so did he. But didn't it change the whole dynamics of everything from being a colleague to something much more intimate, even if the attraction was only on his side? What a fool he was...

He swung into the long drive of Easterleigh House and drove down the imposing avenue of beech trees. Their leaves were turning to a hint of red and amber, reflecting the coming autumn, and the house stood at the end of the avenue, its golden stone mellow in the dwindling light—magnificent, but in sad need of repair and refurbishment.

Patrick sighed as he drove slowly towards the house—so many memories were there. His early childhood had been so happy—then all of a sudden things had changed and what had been an idyllic life had become miserable and bitter—so much so that he and his brother couldn't wait to leave. But now he was back and perhaps Easterleigh could once again be a happy home and he could save the place for future generations, as his father longed for. But it was going to be difficult and it was not the right time to fall in love with someone like Jandy Marshall.

'So—don't worry about the flood in the kitchen. Clever me got a plumber and sorted it out,' said Lydia as she doled out spaghetti bolognese for Jandy, Abigail and herself. 'And now, we haven't had much of a chance to talk for the past four weeks, with me being on long-haul flights. Tell me what the new registrar's like. I bet it was difficult for you. I know when I'm working on a different shift with new people, it drives me mad when they don't do things my way.'

Lydia was a stewardess with an airline and had a varied work schedule, together with a hectic social life.

Jandy put a forkful of food in her mouth and chewed it reflectively. She wasn't about to tell Lydia that Patrick Sinclair was drop-dead gorgeous or the tragic story of his wife. If Lydia knew he was unattached, she would never hear the end of it. Lydia was longing for her to find a partner.

'He wasn't bad,' she replied cautiously. 'He's good at his job.'

Lydia's eyes gleamed. 'That's a start! How old is he?'

'Thirtyish—he has a little girl,' added Jandy mischievously, to put Lydia off the scent.

'Damn! Where have all the single men gone in that place?'

'They got snapped up—anyway, Lydia, you know I'm off men for good. They really aren't worth the hassle!'

Lydia laughed and started to clear the plates away. 'Wait

till you meet Mr Right—not everyone's like Terry, you know. There are still a few good men out there.' She added mock-severely, 'Anyway, darling, you need someone to look after you and Abigail in your old age…'

'Here,' protested Jandy. 'I'm not quite in my dotage yet—and if I am, so are you!'

Lydia put her tongue out at her sister. 'Cheeky! Look, love, I'll put Abigail to bed—you look a bit bushed. Have a run through those leaflets on places to let. I have to admit the one I described over the phone was probably a bit pricey so that's a no-no.'

Despite her madcap ideas about what they could afford, Lydia was a tower of strength in so many ways, reflected Jandy as she settled down to riffle through what was on offer in the letting market. Lydia was kind and adored Abigail—but one of these days she would meet someone special and go her own way, and, oh, how Jandy would miss her then! As Patrick had said, it was tough being a single parent.

She started to look at the properties advertised but there was nothing suitable in her price bracket. Anyway, she was finding it hard to concentrate, her mind reverting back to Patrick and reliving that moment when every nerve in her body had been kick-started into life again…

Then there was the tragic revelation about his personal life that belied his surface confidence and good humour. But, of course, she too knew what it was like to put on a good face and if she wasn't careful she'd end up feeling sorry for him. Life went on and you had to put the past behind you, and his arrival seemed to have stimulated thoughts about her future that she hadn't had for a long, long time.

* * *

Jandy didn't sleep well that night, her dreams a jumble of scenarios that mostly featured a man with blue eyes and a brilliant smile, yet in the morning she felt wide awake, anticipating the day with a tremor of nervous excitement. She took a little more care with her hair and didn't forget to put on some lipstick and a stroke of blusher on her cheeks.

'What are you like, Jandy Marshall?' she asked herself scornfully. 'Trying to attract a man because you've learned he's not married. Pathetic!'

All the way to the hospital she tried to persuade herself that she wasn't all that bothered whether Patrick noticed her or not really. He was just another colleague, only there for a few months, but she couldn't stop the way her stomach fluttered when she thought of him and she had a sense of unusual excitement about going to work.

She met Karen coming out of one of the cubicles wiping her hands on a paper towel. Karen raised her eyes to heaven.

'It's one of those days, I'm afraid. We've got an elderly patient with dementia from a care home in Delford—can you believe they've sent him in on his own?'

This happened with monotonous regularity: a confused patient would be 'dumped', as Dr Vernon put it, in A and E with little information on his health or age, and it would take considerable time to establish what was wrong with him as he couldn't help with any questions. Karen bustled off to contact the care home and Jandy looked at the list of patients to be discharged.

'That's a familiar name,' she murmured. 'Albert Roper...' She scanned his notes, which informed her that the patient had seen Dr Vernon, who had said Mr Roper could be discharged after his intravenous fluid.

She went into the man's cubicle and took a step backwards when she saw that Mr Roper had pulled out his drip and the stand was lying across the floor. Mr Roper was a regular in A and E and it was clear that this was one of his bad days where alcohol was concerned and that he was in belligerent mood.

'Mr Roper! I'll have to put in another drip, you know, before you go home.'

'Get out!' he shouted. 'I'm not having you meddling with me...it's a disgrace!' This was a fairly regular performance. Jandy said nothing, but reached into the cupboard and took down the equipment needed to reposition the drip—needles, alcohol wipes, a saline flush and a tourniquet.

'Now, stay still, Mr Roper. I've got to put another cannula in your vein,' she said, pulling on a pair of lanolin gloves.

The man looked at Jandy craftily for a few minutes as she tried to find a good vein in the knotted old arm he presented to her. Eventually she managed to get the drip put up, and as soon as she'd hooked it onto the stand he laughed and pulled his arm away. Jandy leapt to save the stand from falling over, tripped over the tubing and a spray of blood went over the whole room, including her clothes.

'Mr Roper!' she croaked, on her knees beside the bed. 'What do you think you're doing?'

'I told you to stop mucking me about,' growled Mr Roper.

'Can I help?'

Jandy looked up from her awkward position on the floor to see Patrick looking down at her with an amused grin.

The shock of pleasure at seeing him clashed with the acute embarrassment of Patrick seeing her at her most undignified. So much for her trying to glam herself up that morning! She scrambled up quickly and looked down wryly at her blood-spattered tunic.

'Mr Roper doesn't like having his drip in,' she explained, then added succinctly, 'Mr Roper comes in regularly for fluid replacement so we know him very well.'

'Ah, I see,' said Patrick. He turned to the glowering man and said mildly, 'Mr Roper, if you don't let us put this drip in you won't be able to go home—you'll probably have to sleep on a trolley all night as we don't have enough beds for everyone.'

Mr Roper considered this for a few seconds, then he said sulkily, 'Put the damn thing in, then—I'm fed up with the lot of you!'

Jandy went out to change her clothes. 'Magic touch, Dr Sinclair,' she murmured as she passed him.

'Just the usual skill,' he said modestly, winking at her.

Tim Vernon was talking to Karen as Jandy came by and raised his eyebrows. 'You've been in the wars,' he remarked.

'Mr Roper wasn't too keen on me putting in his cannula,' she explained. 'Dr Sinclair's persuaded him to have it done, but I'll have to clean up that cubicle.'

Tim sighed and said crustily, 'If I remember the last time Mr Roper came in, the same thing happened. Let me know when he's actually out of the building, will you?' He turned to Karen and stroked the side of his face with a grimace. 'Any aspirins in that drawer of yours, Sister? I've got a devil of a toothache...and I want to go through the admissions with you.'

'Come with me, Doctor—I've got a magic formula to help with that,' said Karen soothingly.

They disappeared into Sister's office and Jandy grinned. Karen had a profusion of 'magic cures' to keep headaches, stomach upsets and other ailments at bay. Tim seemed to suffer more than most from his teeth and it didn't do much for his temper.

Jandy went to change her tunic and then went to a box on the wall with cards of patients waiting to be seen. Just as she was about to take the top card, there was a sudden commotion and two youths, pushing and shoving each other, staggered into the corridor from the waiting room. They were laughing uproariously and taunting other patients in the cubicles. Close on their heels was Danny, face bright red and looking flustered.

'How long have these two been making trouble?' Jandy hissed to Danny as he passed her.

'Too long,' he said breathlessly. 'I've rung Security, but apparently there's trouble in the car park and resources are stretched. I'm still waiting for someone to come. Any minute now there's going to be a bust-up.'

'This is ridiculous,' muttered Jandy, looking around desperately to see if anyone was about. Karen and Tim were in her office and she knew that Bob Thoms was doing a small procedure in one of the theatres.

She went behind the desk and hit the emergency button, which was meant to alert Security that a major incident was happening, then marched up to the young men, who were now making lewd suggestions to each other about a young woman sitting scared and rigid with fear outside a cubicle.

'Could you keep it quiet please and go back to the

waiting room?' she shouted above their deafening voices. 'Which of you is the patient?'

A youth in a leather jacket and trousers liberally festooned with chains and zips stared at her and then said aggressively, 'About time too—we've been waiting hours here.' He pointed to the other lad. 'Les is first in the queue.'

'He's been seen by the triage nurse—there are other people who need more urgent attention.'

The youth swaggered up to her, pushing a finger at her chest aggressively, and the smell of strong beer wafted over her.

'You see Les now...or else.' He looked around at the nervous people in the corridor and snarled, 'This place is a joke—the hospital ought to be reported, keeping us waiting. Les is in agony with his ankle.'

He was standing eyeball to eyeball with Jandy, his face thrust forward, blotchy with the effect of alcohol, his breath stale. Behind him Les raised a ragged jeer.

'Yeah! That's right, Phil—you tell 'er!'

'Les will be seen as soon as possible...you, please go!'

Jandy stood her ground resolutely, inwardly praying that someone from Security would come before the whole place erupted, and wondering what it was about this job that she enjoyed. A baby started wailing in Paediatrics and Phil kicked away a chair near his foot and grabbed Jandy's arm.

'You listen here, my dahlin', unless someone sees us in a minute, I'm going to give you something you won't like.'

'Get your hands off me!' shouted Jandy, beating at him ineffectually with her free hand and kicking his shin as hard as she could. 'Your friend won't be seen at all if—'

He twisted her arm viciously. Jandy lost her balance and

landed with a thump on the floor, a chair he'd kicked to one side just missing her forehead. Then several things happened. A large figure interposed itself between Jandy and the youth and Patrick's voice roared out, 'What the hell do you think you're doing?'

The youth was grabbed by the feet as he tried to run away and landed on his stomach with a loud yell. Two security guards appeared and handcuffed the squirming boy, now emitting colourful expletives, while Jandy still sat on the floor, slightly dazed and watching the evolving scene with amazement. Patrick towered above the boy, staring down at him, gimlet-eyed.

'You got a complaint, son? Put it in writing, then. Meantime, these gentlemen have a few questions to ask you, I'm sure!'

The youth looked up at him sullenly. 'It's a disgrace. I've bust my nose…' he started to say.

'Is that all you've bust? A pity!' Patrick's face was grim and flinty-eyed. 'Can't you read?' He pointed to a sign on the wall. 'It says there that any aggression towards members of staff will lead to prosecution—and this little episode's all on video too. It won't make pretty viewing.'

Les snarled, although he took a step backwards from Patrick's menacing figure.

Patrick folded his arms and glared at them. 'Your friend may be seen if he remembers his manners. You—get moving! Oh, and Security will answer any questions you might have.'

Les turned round sulkily. 'They're a bunch of losers here,' he shouted vaguely to the stunned onlookers, trying not to lose face by having the last word.

He shuffled out, leaving his mate sitting hunched on a

chair, staring at the floor. An old man peered out of one of the cubicles and shouted in a quavery voice, 'Well done, sir! That sort need birching, the lot of them!'

'What's going on?' asked Tim, appearing out of Karen's office. 'There's been a lot of a noise…'

'Under control now, I think, Dr Vernon,' said Patrick. 'Staff Nurse has just taken the brunt of some unwanted visitors.'

'You all right, Staff?' Tim asked with concern. 'We really need to up the security in this place if people are getting through here so easily from the waiting room. Go and take her for a coffee, Patrick—I'll beep you if you're needed.'

Patrick squatted down by Jandy. His voice had lost the steely tones he'd used on the youths and now he said drily, 'This is the second time I've found you lying on the floor in about twenty minutes. You landed with an almighty thump—are you OK?'

'Fortunately I landed on my bottom—it was just a bit of a shock,' remarked Jandy. She grinned rather shakily up at him. 'Just a normal day in Casualty. I should be used to it by now, but I was a bit slow off the mark and didn't see it coming.'

'Promise me one thing,' Patrick said sternly. 'Don't try and take on those thugs again.'

He looked at her fiercely and she laughed. 'I'm a big girl now, Patrick, big enough to look after myself!'

Without a word he stooped down and slipped his arms under hers, lifting her effortlessly to her feet. In the second that he pulled her up they were facing each other, her body brushing against his broad frame, her face inches away from his. She could see the dark flecks in his blue eyes, a red mark on his cheek where he'd cut himself shaving. A giggle threatened to burst out of her mouth—if they hadn't been in the hospital she might have thrown caution to the wind and pulled him down towards her!

He placed her gently on a chair and then put a hand on each arm of the chair, preventing her from getting up, and looked down at her with amusement in those beguiling blue eyes. 'Leave the strong-arm tactics to Security next time, all right?'

'OK, OK. And, Patrick…thank you very much.'

She spoke lightly but a sudden chill of caution laid its fingers on her heart—she wasn't a fool. She was being drawn inexorably to Patrick Sinclair. Every time she saw him she longed to touch him, lean against his athletic body. If she wasn't careful she'd be imagining a happy-ever-after scenario. She knew without a doubt that the attraction she felt towards him was more than a just a mild and diverting flirtation—it was real and powerful. She shivered slightly. She'd allowed one man to rule her heart and dominate her and it had ended in bitter tears because she'd trusted him. She couldn't allow herself to fall into that trap again.

She stood up resolutely. 'Back to work,' she said breathlessly. 'I'm fine now.'

He shook his head. 'Not before you've had a strong cup of coffee—Tim Vernon suggested it, and you need a breather.' He shot a look at his watch. 'Perhaps we've time to talk about that property I know about for rent and organise something for our daughters to do together.'

She opened her mouth to say she was quite OK and didn't need a coffee, but she made the mistake of looking into those blue amused eyes of his. She needed somewhere to live, didn't she? For Lydia and Abigail's sake she'd have a coffee with him...

'That would be lovely,' she said meekly.

CHAPTER FOUR

THE canteen had the familiar smell of chips mingled with roast meat, and was teeming with people shuffling along in the queue. The staff sat in a section behind a screen covered with plastic flowers and there were two huge tubs of dusty-looking plastic palms at the entrance.

'Don't say I don't ask you to the most exotic places,' said Patrick drily to Jandy. 'Bag two seats in the corner, and I'll get something wonderfully delicious from the machine to save us queuing up.'

Jandy watched him weaving his way back to her through the tables a couple of minutes later, concentrating on balancing two plastic cups and chocolate bars in his hands. He looked impressively tall and imposing in that sea of people and she could see Tilly pointing him out to the little group of student nurses she was sitting with. No doubt she was telling them that Patrick Sinclair was the greatest thing since sliced bread! Funny, thought Jandy, how she felt like she'd known him for ages, though in reality it had only beena week or so.

'Right,' he said, easing himself into his seat. 'Have a reviver.' He took a sip of his own coffee and grimaced.

'Ah—nectar,' he remarked dourly. 'Although I'd put more emphasis on the "tar" myself…'

She giggled, feeling a sudden light-heartedness in his company, and he grinned back at her. 'Now, tell me honestly if you feel OK after that oaf knocked you down,' he said.

Jandy smiled ruefully. 'Only slightly shaky. I promise you it was only my pride that was hurt. I'm just annoyed that I let him get to me. I ought to have learned by now.'

'I take it there's an assault book to record this sort of thing?'

Jandy nodded. 'It's usually full after two weeks. Anyway, I'm glad that you turned up when you did.'

'So am I. It's a familiar story, though, isn't it? Aggression fuelled by drink and drugs.' Then he shrugged. 'There's not much we can do about it apparently. Anyway, to change the subject…' He reached into his jacket pocket and drew out a piece of paper, unfolding it in front of Jandy. 'Perhaps you'd like to see the place I was telling you about that's available for rent.'

She looked with interest at the photo of a small house, unusual in aspect with an octagonal shape and two dormer windows in the roof.

'It looks really quaint—rather like a little gingerbread house!' she exclaimed. 'I'd love to look around it. Although,' she added cautiously, 'it all depends on the rent, to be truthful…'

'It's not been lived in for a while—it needs a clean and a bit of decoration, so the rent isn't all that high. Frankly, you'd be doing the owner a favour if you decide to take it.'

It sounded almost too good to be true. So many things had been a battle for her in recent years, from finding childcare for Abigail to getting a job she loved, that suddenly being offered what looked like a lovely little house was almost unbelievable. She felt a sudden lump of gratitude in her throat and said in a muffled voice, 'It would be such a load off my mind to get somewhere soon—I have to admit I'm really getting desperate. My priority, of course, is Abigail and I just can't sleep thinking we won't have a roof over our heads....'

Patrick looked at her perceptively, her lovely eyes bright with tears, aware of the emotion in her voice and the fact that Jandy had been hiding a lot of stress behind her bright manner.

'If you want to look around it this weekend, I could arrange to get the key—if it suits you, it's yours!'

Jandy heaved a huge sigh. 'I'm so grateful to you.' She gave a shaky laugh. 'I really thought I'd never get anywhere suitable so quickly—I imagined us camping out on the street!'

Patrick smiled, lowering his glance to give her time to compose herself. 'Let's hope it fits the bill, then,' he said.

'Does it belong to a friend of yours?' Jandy asked.

Patrick hesitated briefly then said, 'It's owned by a relative and I know he's very keen to have it occupied. I'll give you the directions and meet you there at about ten-thirty on Saturday morning.'

Jandy's heart gave a leap of pleasure and relief that her worries about getting some accommodation might be solved, and also that in a few days she would be seeing Patrick outside the confines of the hospital...

'That would be great, although I'll probably have to bring Abigail with me, if that's OK.'

'Then I'll bring Livy.' He smiled. 'They can give us their

opinion of the place and they can meet each other!' He pushed a large chocolate biscuit towards her. 'Here—it's not much, but it might keep you going till lunchtime.'

'Thanks. I can't resist it, I'm afraid, although I am trying to cut out chocolate,' she remarked, unwrapping it and biting into it hungrily.

Blue eyes flicked over her. 'I don't know why,' he murmured. 'I wouldn't have thought you had any weight issues.'

Jandy laughed. 'You should see me with nothing on— I'm awfully...' She stopped, suddenly realising what she'd said, and blushed, the thought of him seeing her stark naked a little too intimate to contemplate.

Patrick raised his brows and his eyes twinkled. 'I'm sure there's nothing awful about you, but if you like I'll give you a medical assessment...'

'I don't think so!'

'Well, the offer's there—only too pleased to give you my professional opinion!' He grinned, leaning back in his chair looking at her with amusement, and their eyes locked, an unmistakeable spark of attraction and intimacy flicker-ing between them: Jandy dropped her eyes and inspected a split nail rather thoroughly and tried to smother a giggle.

There was a second's silence, Patrick's gaze roving over her, then he said hesitantly, 'Perhaps I shouldn't ask this, but you mentioned that you were a single parent but not a widow...does that mean you and your husband are divorced?'

Jandy's expression changed and he put up his hand in apology. 'I'm sorry—please don't answer that. It's nothing to do with me.'

She stared at the table and folded the biscuit wrapper

into a precise square. Was she ready to reveal her sad little story to someone she'd only known for a short time? It made her seem so gullible, so easily deceived—and incredibly stupid to have become pregnant, believing that Terry would have been as thrilled as she was to have their baby. But it was a long time ago now and quite a few people knew her background anyway, so why shouldn't Patrick be told?

She gave a little shrug and said at last, 'It's not a secret, Patrick. I was a naïve fool and fell for someone who was already married with a family—although I didn't realise that at the time.'

Patrick looked at her in horror. 'How did you find out?'

'When I discovered I was pregnant and told him, thinking he'd be delighted as he'd often told me how fond of children he was, he took fright and blurted out the truth.' Jandy's eyes narrowed, and she unconsciously twisted her hands together. 'I can remember his precise words actually. He said, "You idiot! I can't possibly have a child. I realised you were getting too sweet on me recently."'

Patrick shook his head. 'He sounds unbelievable!'

'Ah—but listen to the punchline he gave,' Jandy added succinctly. '"I've already got a wife and two daughters, which is quite enough to cope with!" Shortly after that he disappeared into the blue yonder, leaving me to cope alone.'

'What an idiot!' Patrick's voice was rough with disgust.

Jandy shrugged and said firmly, 'Actually, it taught me a lesson—never fall in love with someone who's carrying a lot of baggage. There won't be room in his life for him to concentrate on anyone else. I suspected Terry had other things in his life but I didn't realise that it was a ready-grown family!'

An unreadable expression suddenly crossed Patrick's face and he nodded slowly. 'You're right. You couldn't risk going through that again—you must have been through hell.'

'I'm over it now. Terry's history as far as I'm concerned, and although I wish he was around for Abigail sometimes, I think we're really better off without him.'

'So he's never contributed anything towards Abigail's upbringing?' asked Patrick softly.

Jandy looked at him levelly. 'I don't want anything from that man. He lied to me for the six months we went out with each other, convincing me that he loved me and wanted a future with me.' She added semi-jokingly but with a touch of sadness, 'I was totally naïve, but I could never go through the roller-coaster of emotions again that I went through with Terry—it took too long to recover!'

And I wonder if she's really recovered now, thought Patrick, sipping the remains of his coffee and watching her face over the rim of his cup. There was a wistful expression in her eyes. The wound might have healed, but it had left a scar that would probably affect her for many years. And couldn't that scar be reopened if she was hurt again by someone who was wary of committing wholeheartedly to a relationship, someone who already had plenty of responsibilities…someone like him, for instance? Didn't he fit into that category?

'I guess this happened in Manchester, then. And when you had Abigail, you came back here?' he said quietly.

Jandy nodded. 'I met Terry in Manchester, but he disappeared after I turned down his suggestion to have an abortion. I've never seen or heard from him since.'

'He sounds charming,' remarked Patrick with heavy irony.

'I went to stay with my mother who lives in Scotland, and had the baby there.' She laughed. 'Mum was wonderful, but she has her own life—namely living with a garage mechanic who's half her age! I realised after a few weeks that having a daughter and a grandchild living with you in a tiny house doesn't fit into the love-nest scenario!'

'So you moved back here?' Patrick murmured.

'Yes, I came back here with Abigail and set up home with my sister. She's a tower of strength and we get on very well. And then I went back to nursing. It's a busy life, but Abigail is secure and happy—and, of course, she's my priority. It's important that she has stability in her life— a proper home, not a stopgap until I can get something permanent.'

Patrick nodded. 'You must have been having a few sleepless nights,' he murmured.

He leant back in his chair and looked at Jandy perceptively—the determined tilt of her chin, the steady look of purpose in her eyes. He admired the way that she had managed to get her life on an even keel again despite all her difficulties—his offer of the house would be a godsend to her. But he hadn't realised the ghastly story behind the fact that she was a single parent. How cruel would it be to risk upsetting her little boat and drawing her into his complicated life? If she took the house they would be bound more closely together—and would that be wise?

'And what made you take up nursing?' he enquired lightly, changing the subject.

Jandy smiled. 'Someone gave me a nurse's outfit when I was little, and somehow the idea of becoming a real nurse got a hold of me. I must have been mad—it's hard to bring up a child on my salary!'

'But you enjoy your work and your sister helps you with your little girl?'

'Yes—I'm very lucky, and Abby adores Lydia. And you?' she asked. 'Was your father a doctor? That often seems to inspire people to take up medicine.'

'No. My father is…well, he's a farmer really and loves the land. I think he'd have liked me to have taken it up too, but my brother and I were impatient to do our own thing.'

'I heard you say you were living with your father?'

'For the time being,' Patrick replied lightly. 'My little girl loves living in the house.'

'And whereabouts…?'

'Oh, not too far away—reasonably convenient.'

There was something about his voice—a studied vagueness—as if he had suddenly pulled the shutters down about any more information on his personal life, and Jandy flicked a look of slight surprise at him. She was perceptive enough to realise that there'd been a slight shift in his attitude towards her—as if he'd stepped back a bit. She felt slightly hurt, as he'd asked her about her past and she'd been frank with him. It seemed he was less eager to confide in her and she'd obviously taken too much for granted. She took the hint and stood up quickly.

'I'll look forward to seeing the house on Saturday, then,' she said briskly. 'And thanks for the coffee and rescuing me from those yobs. I'd better get back or Karen won't be too pleased.'

Patrick toyed with his coffee spoon, watching Jandy go out of the canteen, the light catching her burnished hair, now done up in a neat coil at the back of her head. He'd only known her a week or two, and yet he was beginning to feel he'd known her for many months. They had much in common, and perhaps they could have helped each other heal the wounds they had from the past—but he wasn't ready to commit to anyone yet.

He sighed heavily. If he didn't put the brakes on things, his relationship with Jandy might turn into a rerun of what had happened in London in the months after Rachel had died.

Gazing unseeingly across the table, the ghastly loneliness of that time came flooding back to him, and how easily he'd hurtled into a relationship with someone he'd known only briefly. He'd been vulnerable, hating the thought of being alone, feeling deeply guilty that he had caused his wife's death. Tara had been a shoulder to cry on, deeply sympathetic, limpet-like in her determination not to leave him alone. By the time he had realised he was only desirable to her because of his family background, and that she had absolutely no interest in his little daughter, indeed was irritated by her, it had been almost too late to extricate himself from the engagement he'd been coerced into.

He didn't think that Jandy was the type of girl to be impressed because of who he was—it might even be the reverse. But the fact remained that they were two people with unhappy pasts and he couldn't bear to make another mistake like that, or saddle someone like Jandy with his problems. Was it fair of him to get too close to someone who had been hurt so much already?

He pushed his fingers through his hair distractedly. Why the hell had he mentioned the empty house to Jandy? But now he couldn't in all conscience renege on his offer. He'd promised her she could have the place if she liked it and, besides, now he realised how desperate she was for somewhere reasonable to live. For the sake of her child, he had to keep the offer open—but for the sake of Jandy and himself, he had to stand back a little and not do anything that might bring them into close contact outside the hospital.

Then the beeper in his pocket went off and he stood up and walked briskly back to A and E, trying to push his frustration to the back of his mind.

Saturday morning at last! Jandy helped Abigail put on her little jeans and sweater and brushed her daughter's hair briskly.

'Ow! Stop it, Mummy—I don't need my hair brushed. Ow!'

'Nearly done! There—you look beautiful! We're going to meet another little girl this morning so you want to look good, don't you?'

Abigail looked at her mother witheringly. 'No, I don't! Who is she anyway?'

'I work with her daddy and we're going to look around a house he knows that's for rent—it might be OK for us. It's in the country.'

Abigail perked up. 'I like the country. We could have horses and dogs and cats and—'

'Whoa!' Jandy laughed. 'Wherever we live we can't have animals—we're all out too much. And, of course, the house may not suit us, or it may be too expensive. We'll see.'

It had been a busy week as usual, but every so often in the middle of dressing a wound or calming a screaming child, the thought of her meeting Patrick to see the cottage would flash into her mind and her pulse would bound into excitement. How sad it was that in her dull life meeting someone to look at a house seemed exhilarating!

They got into the car and she drove off towards the cottage.

There was the smell of damp leaves and earth newly turned after the harvest as they got out of the car in the little lane outside the cottage. A little tremor of pleasure darted through Jandy as she gazed at the building. It was quaint, with leaded-paned windows and old tree trunks holding up the roof of the little porch; an old rose twined its way randomly round the front door, a few dying blooms still there. She could easily imagine herself living here, surrounded by fields and the view of the soft Derbyshire hills.

She was surprised to see that the cottage was actually an old gatehouse at the back entrance of an estate, although the drive had long been blocked off and the property stood in its own garden. It was just possible to see a large and imposing mansion through the woods that grew beyond the garden, mullioned windows glittering in the sun. The little village was just down the road, and although it was about six miles from Delford, it would be possible to get to work on time if she got up early. There was even a little village school that Abigail could attend when she was old enough. She turned to Abigail, who was standing at the gate of the field watching the sheep grazing there.

'Come on, poppet, let's go into the garden and wait for Patrick there. He should be here in a minute.'

Jandy looked around with pleasure. So far, so good. There was a neat little garden with room enough to play but not so huge that she'd have to spend every weekend gardening. She turned round as she heard a car stopping outside the gate and Patrick and his daughter arrived. If Tilly could see him now, she'd probably be speechless, reflected Jandy as she watched him walk towards her. Casual suited Patrick—dark cords and a thick cream Arran sweater with an old scarf round his neck made him look rugged and—no getting away from it—very sexy!

The little girl by his side had auburn hair springing round her head like a halo, and looked very like the photograph of her mother that Jandy had seen.

'And I guess this is Livy?' Jandy said, smiling down at the child. 'Meet my little girl, Abigail—you're both the same age.'

The two children stared at each other cautiously then Patrick took out a key and opened the front door.

'In you go, girls—see what you think and then tell us!'

Jandy watched the children run inside and smiled at Patrick. 'What a beautiful little girl Livy is—she looks so much like her mother in the photo I saw.'

'Yes,' he said simply. 'She's the image of Rachel—every time I see her I'm reminded of her mother.'

The sadness in his voice revealed a lot, thought Jandy. It wasn't that she didn't expect him to still feel deeply about Rachel, but it seemed clear to her that Patrick's allegiance still belonged in the past to a wife who had died.

'Right!' she said brightly, stepping into the front room. 'I hope Abigail doesn't fall too heavily for the house because it may be way above my budget.'

He nodded. 'I have been wondering if it's suitable after all. It's in a bit of a mess and the bedrooms are very small.'

'Ah, well, a lick of paint does wonders for a place, doesn't it?'

The front door led straight into a little front room with wallpaper hanging in strips from the walls and plaster from the ceiling in little heaps on the floor. But it was cosy with a pretty bay window that let in the light and through which there was a wonderful view. Jandy could just imagine herself sitting in that bay, basking in the warmth of the sun. She turned to Patrick.

'So far I love it,' she said, with a delighted smile.

He frowned slightly. 'You do? Better reserve judgement until you've seen upstairs.'

Abigail and Livy were running in and out of the two small bedrooms with lots of giggles, hiding in a cupboard on the landing and jumping out—they had obviously made friends with each other.

'Look, Mummy, I can have this room—it's got a little mouse's nest by the fireplace. Isn't that sweet?' cried Abigail, taking her mother's hand and dragging her round the room.

'I think he'd be happier living in the field where he came from,' said Jandy firmly. 'Anyway, you and I will have the bigger room and Lydia will have that room as there's only one of her. And actually we haven't decided to have it yet.'

'No—you don't want to make a hasty decision,' put in Patrick quickly. 'There are disadvantages to living out in the country.'

Jandy flicked a look at his face—there was something uneasy about his expression. Suddenly she guessed that he was regretting mentioning the house to her. He certainly sounded very negative all of a sudden about the whole thing. She wasn't about to be put off, whatever he thought.

'There are drawbacks about living in Delford too,' she pointed out. 'The traffic, the noise, the crime…it could be a wonderful move to leave that behind.'

He nodded sombrely. 'That's true. But you live with your sister—won't she want to look at it too?'

'Oh, I assure you Lydia will like anything I like. We generally have very similar tastes—except when it comes to spending money! Anyway, she's away with her job quite a bit and she's happy to leave it all to me.'

Abigail came running back to Jandy and looked up at her pleadingly. 'I love it here—please let's live here. I could have a rabbit. Livy says she'd look after it for me, and she only lives just up the road—we're neighbours!'

'Oh, I see…' Jandy turned to Patrick with surprise. 'I didn't realise you lived so close by.'

'I'm not all that far away,' he admitted. Again that dismissive tone of voice, keeping her at a distance.

Jandy felt a flash of irritation. Why couldn't the man say just exactly where he lived—what was the mystery? Well, she wasn't going to be put off renting a place that he had suggested so enthusiastically a short time ago, just because he was having cold feet.

'I do like the place,' she said decisively. 'Perhaps we could discuss terms and conditions and if they're OK then I'd like to go ahead.'

'Right,' said Patrick heavily. 'Come downstairs and I'll go over it with you.'

It didn't take long to discuss and Jandy readily agreed the rent. In all conscience, Patrick had to quote the market price for the property, although he'd been tempted to ask more than he thought Jandy could afford in the hope that she wouldn't take it. However much he longed to get closer to her, he was in no position to jump into a relationship at the moment.

He looked at her profile as she read the agreement for the rent of the house, and noted the endearing habit she had of biting her bottom lip when she was concentrating on something. God, he thought wistfully, she was beautiful and completely unconscious of her looks. Her sherry-coloured eyes were warm and sparkled when she was animated, and her hair, usually tied back at work, fell like a golden bell against her neck, brushing against the collar of her blouse.

How was he going to avoid seeing her when she was going to be living so close to him—or stop himself from coming round to see how she was? It would be very easy to get entangled in her life. He'd just have to be disciplined, he thought grimly. Keep work and home separate.

She looked up at him with those wide brown eyes, and smiled happily. 'I know my sister will love this place as much as I do—and I can't wait to move in!'

'Then I hope you'll be very happy here,' he said rather stiffly.

'And when we're straight, you must come and have a meal with us to celebrate,' Jandy said pleasantly.

He longed to say how much he'd enjoy that but felt he had to backpedal, keep his distance, and not show too much enthusiasm.

'Some time perhaps, but I've a very full schedule at the moment.'

He sounded dismissive of her well-meant invitation and Jandy felt a sting of resentment. She certainly wouldn't ask him again!

He turned round quickly, almost relieved as the two little girls clattered into the room. 'Right, Livy, off we go! I've a million things to do this morning!'

'Oh, Daddy, can't Abigail come and play with me? I could show her my pony.'

Both children looked hopefully up at him, but he shook his head and said peremptorily, 'Sorry, not today—it's completely out of the question. We'll see Abigail soon perhaps. Come on, now!'

His voice was curt, and Livy's lips turned down at his sharp tone, but Patrick took her hand and led her firmly out to the car, and in a few seconds he'd accelerated off down the road, with the barest of goodbyes. He looked in the mirror as he drove off and could see Jandy staring after him, an expression of surprise on her face, and groaned. He must have sounded rude. It saddened him to hurt her, but surely he was right to stand back a little, put on the brakes? He had too many issues to deal with—not only his sensitivity about his background but about his life back in Delford.

He changed gear roughly so that the car jolted. How simple life would have been without the ties of Easterleigh and his family!

'I like Abigail, Daddy—and I like Jandy. Can they come and see us soon…please? They're nice, aren't they?' piped up Livy's little voice from the back of the car.

'Very nice, darling,' said Patrick heavily. 'Perhaps in a few weeks when they've settled in.'

* * *

Jandy frowned in bewilderment as she watched the car disappear round the corner. What on earth had she done wrong that he should leave so abruptly? It had been his idea to show her the cottage, yet suddenly he seemed to be backpedalling as if he wanted as little to do with her as possible. There was no mistaking his churlish manner. Perhaps, she thought sadly, he didn't seem quite such a nice guy after all. Perhaps her sordid little tale about Abigail's father had put him off in some way.

Abigail started to cry. 'Why couldn't I go with Livy? It's not fair! I want to see her pony. Why wouldn't her daddy let her?'

Why wouldn't he indeed? Jandy closed the garden gate and opened the car door for Abigail to get in. Even though she realised his wife still held a treasured place in his heart, Jandy was as sure as anything that there had been a mutual attraction between Patrick and her. Surely it hadn't been all in her imagination?

It was a warning for her not to assume anything, she reflected bitterly as she clicked Abigail's car seat belt into place. He wasn't the affable man he seemed to be—that was for sure. She should steer well clear of him. The light-heartedness she'd felt over the past weeks since she'd met Patrick began to evaporate.

'When we live here, Mummy, can Livy come and play again?' Abigail pleaded.

'Perhaps, Abigail—we'll have to see,' sighed Jandy, glancing in her mirror and moving off slowly down the road.

Blast the man. His attitude seemed to have dampened her excitement in finding a lovely place at the right price. Then she shrugged. She damn well wasn't going to be downhearted. His manner was inexplicable, but she'd get over it. She'd had enough of moody men and their hang-ups.

'Don't worry, Abigail,' she reassured her little daughter. 'We're going to have lots of fun in our new little home!'

CHAPTER FIVE

A FEW days later Jandy switched on the TV and flopped back on the sofa. The news was on, with the usual catalogue of financial disaster and celebrity mishaps. She let it wash over her, allowing herself to relax after a busy week of trying to get rid of some of the junk she didn't need when she moved, culminating in a very tough day at the hospital.

A terrible road crash involving a coach party of pensioners on the motorway had resulted in two fatalities and multiple serious injuries and had occupied all the staff in A and E for many hours. Most of the people involved would feel the effects for the rest of their lives. Of course, that was the nature of the job, but no matter how experienced you were it was hard not to get involved emotionally and block out the graphic pictures of terrible wounds and grief that dominated that kind of scenario—it remained with you for a long time. She took a deep draught of the glass of chilled Bordeaux she had in her hand, welcoming the anaesthetising effect after a traumatic few hours.

Jandy's thoughts drifted back over the day and inevitably to Patrick. There was no doubt about it. Since he had left so abruptly from the cottage he was less than forthcoming—quite distant, in fact, although they hadn't been working together all the time and there hadn't been many opportunities for chat. Today he'd been part of the team looking after the crash victims, not only with the practical elements of trying to resuscitate a dying man but he'd also had to tell the weeping daughter that her father had died. He had done it with compassionate and gentle understanding that had belied his tough exterior.

But she couldn't help puzzling over Patrick's change of attitude. He had seemed so sympathetic, so understanding, so comforting when she'd told him that she was a single parent. He understood only too well what it was to lose love. Then that warmth had evaporated like mist on a warm day after she'd divulged the full story of Terry's betrayal to him over coffee. She'd tried to put the whole episode out of her mind—but it hurt, no doubt about that.

Bleakly she took another sip of wine and stared blankly at the screen, lost in her thoughts, vaguely aware that the programme was now the local news. An elderly, rather frail man in a wheelchair was being interviewed by a young woman, and they were standing in front of a large mansion with golden stone and red Virginia creeper winding its way over the walls. Jandy recognised it immediately as the stunning house she had seen through the trees behind the little cottage the other day, and she turned up the volume, interested to hear what was being said about what was, in effect, her neighbour's property.

'Further to our programme on green issues, we are now at Easterleigh House, the magnificent 16th-century home of Viscount Duncan,' said the reporter. She turned to the old man. 'My Lord, you and your son are planning to develop a wind farm on the hills at the edge of your estate. Aren't you worried about the impact of the beautiful views across the countryside—views that have remained the same for centuries?'

'I don't think their impact on the view will be too detrimental, and the fact is that the house and estate needs a great deal of renovation, and we need the income,' replied Viscount Duncan.

'That's an enormous project,' remarked the interviewer.

The old man smiled, and for a moment he reminded Jandy of someone—but she couldn't put her finger on who it was. 'I'm lucky that my son has come home to oversee everything. He's got much more energy than I have! I want to save the place for future generations, and to continue to give employment to people whose families have worked on the farm and land for many years.'

'It's a huge estate,' said the young woman. 'Could you not sell off some of the land to raise money instead of putting up wind farms?'

Lord Duncan frowned and said fiercely, 'I feel it is held in trust. The land was added to over the years by marriages between the local aristocracy—people who loved it, understood it and who were born to look after it, like me. I don't think it should be sold off to just anyone!'

What a snobbish old fossil he is, thought Jandy, amused by his reference to the 'local aristocracy', and his dismissal of other people as 'just anyone'! And yet she could sympathise with his longing to keep his beautiful estate intact.

The young woman turned back to the camera with a bright smile. 'So there you have it—is Lord Duncan justified in his scheme? We'd like your comments on what you, the viewers, think about the wind farm. Is it worth saving a stately home to have this project on our doorstep and changing the face of this little corner of Derbyshire? And do you think it will be a positive contribution to the green energy problem? Please let us know!' Then she added brightly, 'And if you're interested in seeing this beautiful old house at close quarters, there's a village fair being held in the grounds here at the weekend in aid of the village hall—so why not come along?'

Jandy yawned and flicked the 'off' button—she was too tired to apply her mind to questions about green issues, although it was mildly interesting that her neighbour was a nobleman. She rinsed her wineglass clean under the tap before she went up to bed, but she was sure she would not sleep well.

A lovely crisp autumn day—and a Saturday, which meant that she and Abigail could go out for the morning, thought Jandy with relief. A welcome change from packing cases and sorting through clothes to be thrown out before the move. Abigail's little bike was in the boot and they drove to the new cottage. On such a lovely day it would be a good idea to stroll around the lanes there and get to know the area.

Jandy noticed the entrance to Easterleigh House just before she got to the cottage. A banner strung across the imposing gates before the long winding drive read, 'Open Day at Easterleigh House in Aid of the Village Hall! Fun for all the Family!' A little stream of people were making their way to the house after paying at the gate. Vaguely Jandy remembered it being mentioned on the television programme about the wind farm that she had watched the previous evening.

'Look, Abigail!' she exclaimed as she parked the car by the road. 'Why don't we go and see what's happening there? There might be all kinds of exciting things to do and we could meet some of our new neighbours—perhaps other little boys and girls you could get to know.'

Abigail was enthusiastic and pedalled her bike up the drive, with Jandy walking briskly beside her. What a place to live, reflected Jandy, looking appreciatively at the beautiful trees turning amber and the magnificent facade of the house facing the drive. No wonder Lord Duncan was so passionate about preserving it.

To the side of the house was an enormous lawn, bounded by huge oaks and cedars, and on this were a variety of stalls and little fairground attractions.

'Mummy, look!' yelled Abigail with delight. 'Swings and roundabouts—can I go on them?'

She got off her bike and gave it to Jandy to hold, before dashing over to the swings and waiting patiently in a queue for her mother to join her and pay for the ride. As Jandy walked towards her another child ran over to Abigail and tapped her on the shoulder, and then both children began jumping up and down in excitement. It was Livy! Jandy's heart thumped. Where Livy was, it meant that Patrick was also nearby—and, of course, he lived near here, so it wasn't surprising that they had come as well. Jandy went up to the little girls.

'Hello, Livy, nice to see you!' she exclaimed.

'I wanted you to come.' Livy beamed. 'I asked Daddy if we could tell you to meet us, but he said he didn't think you'd be able to. I'm going to take Abigail to see my pony when she's been on the rides.'

Jandy felt a moment's desolation at Patrick's reaction to his daughter's request—he was obviously determined that the families shouldn't get involved.

'Where is Daddy?' she asked cautiously.

'Oh, he'll be here later. Grandpa's looking after me at the moment.' She looked round and waved to an old man being pushed across the lawn in a wheelchair, whom Jandy immediately recognised as Viscount Duncan, the man she'd seen on television only the night before.

Livy danced over to him, dragging Abigail with her. 'Grandpa! Grandpa! Look, this is my new friend—she's called Abigail and they're going to live in the little cottage!'

Viscount Duncan smiled indulgently, and held Livy's hand. 'How lovely for you, pet, to have a little friend so near.'

From her vantage point near the swings, Jandy stared at him with incredulity. So Viscount Duncan was Patrick's father! She drew in a breath. And this was where Patrick lived, right bang on her doorstep, in a stately home no less! And he'd kept that very secret! But hadn't she known all along that he was from a background of privilege? The clues were all there after all: his restrained but confident manner; his deep, well-modulated voice. It all added up to someone who was used to the best of everything—including a country estate and a lord for a father!

Why hadn't he told her his background? she wondered. Why had he kept a huge part of his personal life secret? They'd had one or two conversations when it would have been appropriate for him to say where he lived and who his father was, just as she had told him about her failed relationship and her own mother. She watched Abigail running round the lawns with Livy and was suddenly jolted by an unpleasant thought. Had Patrick drawn a veil over his connections because he'd discovered her own background was not from the 'local gentry'?

'Perhaps, having heard my sordid story, he thinks I'm just too common for him!' she said angrily to herself. 'His father seemed to imply that he needs good stock to keep the family line going! And Patrick probably agrees with him!'

She scowled ahead of her for a moment, struggling with that thought, and the painful reflection that Patrick was no better than Terry really if that was what he thought— throwing her to one side when he was frightened they would get too close. He was probably on the lookout for a girl from his background—the 'local aristocracy', not one already encumbered with a four-year-old daughter.

Then she sighed. She'd obviously been reading all the wrong signals. He'd realised that she was not part of his world and it would be silly to form a close friendship with her. That hurt—no matter that they'd only had a brief acquaintanceship, she still felt the sting of rejection from a man she'd imagined had felt the same fierce electric attraction between them as she had. But most of all it hurt that he had, in effect, kept the truth about his life to himself, just like Terry had.

Friday night and there was the first hint of the cutting edge of winter cold about the air. Jandy pulled her coat around her as she walked from her car to A and E for her three-night stint on night duty, and wondered if she'd get the decorating done in her little house by Christmas. It was

September now, and they would have to move in anyway in a few weeks, camping uncomfortably in the bedrooms and doing things gradually.

It would have been fun, giving the place a make-over with Lydia's help, but the whole thing had backfired with Patrick's attitude towards her. How could he have turned out to be such an arrogant pig? From where she was, it seemed that pure snobbery was the only reason for his sudden coldness.

Probably, she thought scornfully, his father wielded a lot of influence over him. He'd sounded very Victorian, she would be deemed as highly unsuitable—a single mother with no money, whose own mother lived with a mechanic young enough to be regarded as a toy-boy, just the sort of girl he would advise his son to avoid!

Was she being over-sensitive? Jandy shrugged. Whatever the reason, she would keep her distance for a while and she was very relieved that he wasn't on this weekend night shift. She was thinking far too much about the man, despite her annoyance with him.

'Hi, there,' said Bob, joining her as they walked down the corridor. 'God, I hate this shift—it's the worst of the whole week.'

'Ah, well—it's only for a few days,' commented Jandy absently. 'And then four days off.'

'Three nights of hell...' grumbled Bob, opening his locker and slinging his bag and jacket into it.

Jandy sympathised with him. There were more attempted suicides, more alcohol abuse as drinkers celebrated the end of the working week, and more road traffic accidents on a Friday night—and all sometimes crowded into a small space of time.

On her way to the central desk, Jandy passed an elderly couple walking very slowly to Reception. The woman was supporting the man as he shuffled along, stopping every now and then to draw breath.

'Can I help?' asked Jandy. 'Have you booked in yet?'

'My…my friend doesn't seem able to breathe very well,' said the little old lady, looking anxiously at Jandy. 'We've only just come back from holiday and he started to feel unwell getting off the plane. I got a taxi, although he said it was nothing, and now…'

She stopped speaking and watched in distress as the man slid slowly to the floor and lay there motionless, except for the labouring motion of his chest trying to take in air, his breath stertorous.

'Oh, heavens… Charles, what's the matter?' She bent over him anxiously. 'Oh, dear…'

'Max—bring a wheelchair!' called Jandy sharply to the porter, who as usual, when he hadn't been given anything specific to do, was deep into a detective novel.

'Comin', Nurse—no worry,' he sighed, stuffing the paperback into his back pocket.

Jandy squatted down beside the man and felt his pulse. 'Not too bad—a bit rapid,' she murmured to herself.

The man attempted to sit up and said rather breathlessly, 'I'm all right—I just can't get my breath. I seem to have hurt my leg—it's really painful.'

He sank back with closed eyes and Jandy turned to the elderly lady. 'Has your husband been in pain long?'

'Oh, we're not married,' said the woman quickly, a slight flush of embarrassment on her cheeks. She spoke rapidly, shock making her garrulous. 'We're just very good friends—we were colleagues and we've been on a tour of Greek historical sites.'

'What's your friend's name?' asked Jandy gently.

'Oh, yes, of course… His name's Charles Westhrop. He said his leg was painful as he came down the steps of the aeroplane, and that's about two hours ago, but he won't let me look at it.'

'And your name?'

'Gwen Pendle.'

'Well, I think we'd better look at your friend's leg now, Ms Pendle. Let's get Mr Westhrop into a cubicle.'

Max trundled the wheelchair across and with Tilly's help they managed to get the man onto a bed in the cubicle, and Jandy slipped an oxygen mask over Mr Westhrop's face.

'This should make your breathing easier,' she explained, disguising her shock at the sight of the man's swollen limb as she cut down the trouser leg with a pair of scissors. The skin stretched tight, red and shiny, and she noted the parchment-like pallor of his face and the slight sheen of perspiration on his forehead. He was obviously very ill.

She touched the leg very gently and Mr Westhrop flinched, biting his lip. 'A little painful, that,' he mumbled from behind the mask.

'Tilly, ask Mr Vernon or Dr Thoms to come immediately, would you?' Jandy's voice sounded calm, belying the danger signals that were flashing in her head.

'May I come in?' asked Ms Pendle timidly, putting her head round the curtain.

'Perhaps you'd like to go and have a cup of tea while Mr Westhrop is being examined?' Jandy suggested kindly to little Miss Pendle, who was looking rather grey herself at the glimpse she had of her friend's elephantine limb.

'Oh—please let her stay,' said the man weakly.

Gwen put her hand over Charles's and patted it gently. 'Of course I'll stay,' she said bravely. 'I want to know what they have to say about you, Charles—I'll have a cup of tea in a minute.'

'I'll be fine—it's all a fuss about nothing,' said Charles, his voice muffled through the oxygen mask.

But Jandy could tell that he was relieved that Miss Pendle was staying with him—they were obviously devoted to each other. Then the curtain swished aside and Patrick's tall figure appeared.

'Oh...it's you!' she exclaimed, shocked at his sudden appearance.

Her heart clattered uncomfortably against her ribcage—why had he turned up? She wasn't prepared, hadn't expected to see him, and now here he was in front of her, with his dreamy looks and clean-cut image of a film-star doctor in his hospital greens that couldn't disguise his muscular body—the man who'd actually been very rude to her.

She took a deep breath and thought crossly, Darn it, I'm not going to think of how attractive the man is. If he wants to keep me at arm's length because I'm not classy enough for him, that's fine with me!

'I didn't know you were in, Dr Sinclair,' she said coolly. If he expected her to turn on a smile, he had another think coming.

There was something in those deep blue eyes that she couldn't interpret when he glanced at her, then he said briskly, 'Sorry—you'll have to put up with me, I'm afraid. Dr Thoms is busy with a compound fracture at the moment and Mr Vernon's off with a tooth abscess. Now, what have we here?'

'This is Mr Westhrop and his friend, Ms Pendle. He's just come off a long flight from Greece,' explained Jandy crisply. 'He's finding it difficult to breathe and, as you can see, his leg's very swollen and painful. He's been like this for just over an hour since the plane landed. His BP's up and he's got a slight temperature.'

Patrick examined the leg carefully, noting how far the swelling went up the limb.

'This looks like a DVT—a deep vein thrombosis,' he said at last. 'We'll need a duplex ultrasound scan to get a complete diagnosis and pinpoint the exact position of the clot.'

'Do you think it's serious, Doctor?' asked Gwen timidly.

'Potentially it is serious,' explained Patrick honestly. 'Blood clots below the knee we usually regard as non-life-threatening, although they need monitoring. Those clots occurring in the knee's popliteal vein or veins above the knee are more serious.' He turned to Jandy. 'From the look of this leg, Staff Nurse, I would think the clot could be in the iliac vein going right up to the thigh.'

Mr Westhrop gave a little chuckle and pulled his mask away for a moment. 'You always say I don't like to do things by halves, Gwen—now it seems I have something quite dangerous!'

Ms Pendle shook her head at him. 'Charles, you always make light of everything. What can be done to get rid of this clot, then?'

'The body's natural process of clot breakdown, or fib-rinolysis, will eventually help to get rid of it, but I'm going to get a vascular consultant to look at the leg. He may inject an anti-coagulant drug to disperse the clot so that it doesn't end up in an unsatisfactory place, like the lung.'

'Can I go home, then?' asked Charles.

'Not just yet, I'm afraid. We need to prevent further clots occurring and you'll probably be put on some fairly powerful drugs. We'll have to monitor you pretty carefully for the next few days.'

Mr Westhrop digested this information for a moment then said worriedly, 'Oh, dear, I'm due to give a lecture on Greek temples this week and I've got to assemble my notes…'

'I'm afraid that this isn't a minor matter, Mr Westhrop. You have to realise just how serious it is.'

'But the lecture's most important, isn't it, Gwen?' he protested.

Little Ms Pendle stood up, her small figure looking much more authoritative. 'Don't be ridiculous, Charles! Putting a silly lecture before your health. I won't have it! You look terribly ill. You'll stay in hospital until they've got you better…' Her voice wobbled suddenly and she pulled a hanky out of her pocket and blew her nose. 'Giving me all this worry… I couldn't bear it if anything happened to you.'

Everyone in the room looked at the elderly lady in surprise at this unexpected outburst, then Charles smiled and took her hand in his, squeezing it gently. 'My dear, don't get upset—I promise I'll do as I'm told.'

The two old people gazed at each other then Mr Westhrop turned to Jandy and Patrick and said weakly but very firmly, 'I wonder if you kind people would leave us for a minute? I have something very urgent I need to say to Miss Pendle. I'll call you in very soon, I promise.'

Patrick and Jandy stood slightly apart outside the cubicle, both of them maintaining a distance, both of them
acutely aware of each other. Patrick longed to say to Jandy
that he was sorry if he had been very offhand the other day
when she'd agreed the lease of the cottage, and Jandy could
feel the hairs of her neck prickling at his closeness.

She looked at his tall figure under her eyelashes, and
in her imagination she could almost feel his touch—the
roughness of his chin against her cheek, the strength of
his arms holding her against his body. Then she pushed
those thoughts away crossly and tried to dwell only on the
fact that he was a complete snob who had, in a way, misled
her about his background, and she wanted nothing more
to do with him.

At length Patrick said diffidently, 'Mr Westhrop had
better not take long—I don't like the look of that leg at all.
What on earth can he be saying to Miss Pendle?'

'I really have no idea,' said Jandy coldly. She could be
just as stand-offish as he could!

Then Ms Pendle drew back the curtain, looking rather
flushed, and said in a breathless voice and with a little giggle,
'You can come in now. We…we've something to tell you.'

Patrick and Jandy looked at her in mystification. 'What
is it?' asked Jandy.

Charles struggled to sit up, then explained with a little
smile, 'I'll be brief! For many years Gwen and I have been
great friends as well as colleagues. Over time I began to
realise that what I felt for Gwen was more than friendship—in fact, to tell you the truth, I knew that I loved her
very much.'

Patrick's and Jandy's eyes met briefly in a look of astonishment at Mr Westhrop's revelations. Then he took Gwen's hand again and drew her nearer to him.

'It…it never seemed the right moment to tell her, although I've always been longing for an opportunity,' he said softly. 'But suddenly I've just had an epiphany and realised that I'm not immortal and that we may not have much more time to enjoy ourselves. The thing is…' He looked shyly at the elderly lady. 'The thing is, I thought that it was now or never. I've just told Gwen it's about time we got married!'

There was a stunned silence in the room then Jandy broke the silence, clasping her hands in delight and exclaiming, 'What a lovely idea! And how wonderful that you chose to tell us about it!'

'Congratulations, sir—and to you, Ms Pendle,' said Patrick with a grin. 'Who says hospitals aren't romantic places?'

Jandy looked at Gwen. Suddenly she didn't seem like a rather plain elderly lady any more—she looked quite beautiful, lit by an aura of pure happiness. That was what love did to you, Jandy thought wistfully, it made you glad to be alive. It had been a long time since she had felt that bubbling excitement—until the last few days that was… She flicked a quick look at Patrick under her lashes. Hadn't he woken a few emotions that she'd thought had vanished for ever? She bit her lip, and forced herself back to reality and Mr Westhrop's deep vein thrombosis.

'And now I'm going to have to bring you down to earth, I'm afraid,' Patrick was saying. 'We're going to run a barrage of blood tests on you, Mr Westhrop, so perhaps, Ms Pendle, you can go and drink a toast to you and your fiancé with the finest tea our canteen has to offer while we attack him!'

Charles smiled. 'You can do what you like, young man—I may feel awful physically, but I can tell you I've never been happier in my life! You see, I never thought I'd find love at my time of life—and there it was, waiting round the corner. I've spent many years wishing I'd had the courage to ask Gwen to marry me. What a fool I've been! And if it hadn't been for this damn leg I might never have plucked up the courage!' His eyes twinkled at them. 'Let it be a lesson to you young ones never to put off tomorrow what you can do today!'

For a brief second Patrick's gaze swept over Jandy, then he smiled at Charles. 'I'll try and remember what you said, sir,' he murmured.

Max appeared at the door, his kindly face beaming. 'I've come for Mr Westhrop—they're ready to give him his scan now.'

The patient was wheeled away to the X-ray department and Patrick murmured, 'No one can say A and E is dull, that's for sure.' There was a certain awkwardness in his manner, as if he was aware that things weren't easy between them.

'Nice to have a happy ending,' Jandy said coolly, not wanting to be drawn into a discussion with him. 'They're a lovely couple.'

A short silence, then Patrick said abruptly, 'Mr Westhrop's right, of course.'

Jandy looked at him questioningly. 'In what way?'

'Never put off till tomorrow something you can do today…'

Jandy walked back into the cubicle and pulled off the paper sheet to replace it with a fresh one for the next patient. She didn't say anything.

'I'm afraid I owe you an apology, Jandy,' he said softly, following her into the cubicle.

Jandy smoothed out the sheet, her face impassive, belying the surprise she felt. 'How do you mean?'

Patrick sighed. 'Last week…I was damned rude to you. I left without as much as a goodbye—you must have thought it was rather odd, rushing away like that. But I've had time to think about it and—'

Jandy turned round to face him and said candidly, 'I did wonder what I'd done wrong. You suddenly seemed to backtrack on me taking the house…' She held his gaze with hers. 'I got the feeling you didn't really want me to take it—am I right?'

He shook his head and put his hands on her shoulders, his expression contrite. 'I was nervous about you taking on the cottage for various reasons,' he admitted. 'You'd done nothing wrong…it was me, being far too cautious.'

Jandy stood stock still, trying to ignore the electric touch of his hands and just how close he was to her— close enough to pull her towards him and hold her against his chest. 'I can imagine what your reasons are,' she said glacially.

He looked down at her, surprised. 'You can? And what do you imagine?'

She gave a humourless laugh. 'It's obvious, isn't it? You don't want to get involved socially with me. And you think that if I take the house—which I now realise is on your father's land—we'll start to move in the same circles.'

Patrick looked dumbfounded. 'I'm sorry,' he said slowly, 'I don't have a clue what you mean…'

'Well, it wouldn't do at all, would it? To get too friendly

with someone outside your elevated circle—someone like me—would be a total waste of time!'

'You what?' His blue eyes looked down at her in complete bafflement. 'You think I don't want to see you because of some sort of outdated class distinction? I don't believe this...'

'But it's true, isn't it?' Jandy's beautiful tawny flecked eyes gazed up at him challengingly. 'I saw your father on television the other night and it seemed to me he has some pretty feudal ideas, which I imagine have rubbed off on you as well, archaic as they are!'

He nodded as if understanding what she was getting at. 'Ah, so that's it! You saw the programme and you're reading things into it...'

'Am I? We seemed to be getting on pretty well before you heard about my background...an impoverished single parent, and her mother living with a man young enough to be her son. Not very good connections, you might say!'

'Jandy, stop it!' He put a finger over her mouth. 'If I had any reservations about getting "involved socially" with you, I can assure you it was the other way round. I thought the baggage I bring with me isn't something I should involve you in—that was one of the reasons.'

'Easy enough to say. I wish you'd been honest with me. Frankly, I happen to think you're right—we shouldn't be in each other's pockets, and getting involved would be foolish. You live in a different world from me and we wouldn't do for each other at all!'

'That is complete nonsense,' he said angrily, then his face softened. 'Actually, I don't normally tell people now about my background—I find it can get in the way a bit.'

'How?' demanded Jandy tersely.

'Sometimes people want to date me because of who I am, not what I am,' he said drily.

Jandy's eyes sparked across at him, two pink spots of anger on her cheeks. 'Thank you very much—you think I'm as shallow as that do you? I honestly couldn't care less where you come from.'

He groaned, and, putting his hand up to her cheek, turned her face towards him then gently brushed a tendril of hair from her forehead. 'No, I don't think you're shallow, Jandy—but some people are. I'm so sorry—sorry you saw that silly programme and jumped to the wrong conclusions, sorry I've been an idiot. Believe me, there are reasons why I can't involve anyone in my life at the moment.'

She jerked her head away from his hand, and said coldly, 'Apology accepted.' Then she turned to go back down the corridor, wondering exactly where all this had left her. But, of course, she still fancied him like mad, didn't she? Part of her longed to make up with him and to get to know him properly—what made him tick, and what exactly the reasons were that held him back from making any commitment.

Bob stepped out of a cubicle and called after her. 'Fancy a cup of coffee, Jandy?'

Deep in thought, she absently shook her head and walked on, while Bob shrugged and went off by himself to the canteen.

Patrick cursed himself for being such a fool, hurting someone he liked a lot by his clumsy manner. He closed his eyes for a second as the searing guilt of his last words to Rachel came back to him, as they often did when he'd been churlish—a terrible reminder of his tendency to let his temper rule his head. Would he never learn?

Surely he could have kept things between Jandy and himself at a friendly level without offending her, and without allowing them to get too close? As it was, she regarded him as nothing short of a snobbish throwback. He had to try and explain to her, without being specific, why he'd acted as he had—try and convince her that it was to protect her and not him. He wasn't sure she'd believe him, but he hated the thought of being on bad terms with her. In his imagination a pair of eyes the colour of soft amber looked at him reproachfully—and he couldn't stop thinking about them.

CHAPTER SIX

FOR the rest of the weekend there was the usual continuous queue of patients and by Monday morning everyone on the team was exhausted.

'All I want to do is go home and sleep for two days,' sighed Tilly, yawning, slumped with her elbows on the desk.

'Wait till you've done a week of nights,' remarked Jandy, easing her feet out of her shoes surreptitiously. 'I'm going to treat myself to a pedicure soon—my feet don't seem to belong to my body at the moment.'

'Only another hour to go and then home…and then four days off!' Bob stretched and sighed, pinching the skin between his eyes wearily.

And perhaps I can catch up on everything I should have done days ago, thought Jandy. She flicked a look across at Patrick, writing up a patient's report. She had felt acutely conscious of him for the whole weekend, wondering if his apology was just flannel. She'd learned the hard way to be circumspect when it came to believing men. Sometimes, she thought bitterly, it was better to call a halt to your feelings for your own peace of mind. She had clung to the hope for many months that Terry would come back to her, even after she'd had Abigail, unable to break free of the hold he'd had on her. Patrick's attitude to her was a warning for her not to get entangled again with another man who she'd found so instantly attractive. Keep him at arm's length, Jandy, she told herself firmly.

Tim came up to the desk, his face still slightly swollen from the effects of a tooth abscess.

'How are you feeling?' asked Bob.

'I'll be better when the antibiotics have kicked in,' he said, feeling his jaw gingerly. 'I'll be even better when I've had a whisky at home…'

'Not advisable with the antibiotics,' warned Bob.

Tim grinned ruefully, 'Don't take away my only pleasure.' He looked round as he heard the noise of an ambulance drawing up outside the entrance. 'This had better be a minor injury,' he remarked without much hope.

Karen shook her head. 'Just had word that we're to expect two men involved in a fight—one quite serious.'

'If only they could have waited another hour before hitting the daylights out of each other then the next shift could have taken them,' he sighed.

And a few seconds later two stretcher cases were brought in and transferred to casualty trolleys. Tim went over to the first trolley and lifted the blanket from the patient, a burly man with a shaven head and liberally tattooed chest who was emitting deep groans.

Tim took a deep breath and stared at the multiple temporary dressings on the man's arms and legs and a small abrasion on his head.

'This is going to be a long job,' he muttered to Patrick.

'Can you and Staff Nurse get to grips with it while I see to the other patient?'

'That tooth still giving you gyp?' asked Patrick sympathetically.

'Enough to make me a bit woozy on painkillers,' Tim admitted.

Jandy sighed as she pulled on some latex gloves. She would have liked to put a bit of space between herself and Patrick—let the air settle a bit around his apology—but there was no help for it and soon they were standing opposite each other and starting to peel the dressings from their patient. Patrick glanced at her as if about to say something then looked down at the patient, concentrating on the matter in hand.

'What's he called?' Jandy asked the paramedic, as she dropped blood-soaked pads into a bucket.

'Lenny Smith apparently. Got into some sort of fight with a relative,' the man informed them. 'I'll leave you to make him beautiful again—see you!'

'My God,' muttered Patrick, as more of the patient's injuries were revealed. 'What did the other man use to give him these sorts of wounds? Look at all the skin and muscle gouged out of this arm… He's going to need prolonged surgical care after we've contained these injuries.'

'They say heavy spanners are the latest effective weapons,' said Jandy drily. 'Apparently they give a nice variety of wounds…'

'Charming,' remarked Patrick as he and Jandy started to work steadily on the man, swabbing the cuts and gashes, cleaning wounds with badly torn edges on the shins, calves and thighs, and for a short while forgetting about the tension between them as they concentrated. Patrick was painstaking and thorough, closely inspecting the different types of injuries that had been inflicted on the patient. All the wounds were leaking blood profusely.

'It doesn't help that Mr Smith's probably been at the bottle quite hard,' he remarked.

'Is that why he's bleeding so much?' asked Jandy.

Patrick nodded grimly. 'Alcohol certainly makes wounds bleed more freely. Get a sample of blood for cross-matching and set up the clean theatre so that we can do some patching up before he goes to Surgical. He'll need dextran to tide him over until he gets whole blood.'

Jandy went to the theatre used for small operations to lay out the local anaesthetic, dressings and sutures to temporarily deal with the man's injuries and Patrick put on a mask before he started to work closely on the patient. Karen came in to help them.

'I hear this patient's got a few nasty wounds,' she said coming into the clean theatre where small operations were performed.

'I don't know what the other man's like, but Mr Smith's in a shocking state. What were they fighting about?' murmured Patrick to Karen as he started to close the wounds with the soluble sutures that Jandy handed to him.

Karen sighed, her voice tired after twelve hours of demanding work. 'Oh, the usual,' she replied quietly. 'Mr Smith was apparently having it off with his cousin's wife— it doesn't make for happy families, I'm afraid. The other man's got a superficial facial wound, but he's OK.'

Patrick looked up and said sympathetically, 'It's been a long haul, hasn't it? Not long to go now and you can tuck yourselves up for a good sleep in your warm beds!'

'I can't wait,' said Karen as she left the room.

Patrick bent his head over the patient with his back to Jandy, and she looked at his dark hair, slightly too long and overlapping his collar. From her angle he looked quite boyish and vulnerable—someone who wouldn't hurt you intentionally. Perhaps she shouldn't have rejected his apology. After all, he had admitted how rude he'd been.

'Another small threaded needle, please, Nurse,' Patrick said briskly, his voice cutting into her thoughts.

She gave a start and handed him the needle, jerked out of her daydream from contemplating the nape of Patrick's neck and back to reality. She watched him finish suturing the patient, meticulous as he closed the wound with fine silk. After a while he stood back, stretching and putting his hands on his back, trying to knead the muscles he'd strained bending over the man for nearly an hour. Then he peeled off his latex gloves, flung them into the bin and pulled down his mask.

'The wound will probably have to be reopened later to get a better finish—make it cosmetically more acceptable,' he remarked. 'Anyway, I think we've done all we can for Mr Smith now. Tell Max he's ready to go to Surgical.'

She started to leave the room and Patrick touched her arm, his eyes holding hers for a moment. 'Look,' he said urgently. 'Let me make amends for my rudeness—can't we have lunch together in the next few days while we're off? After all,' he coaxed, 'I need to get on with my new neighbour…please?'

Jandy teetered on the brink of agreeing to meet him, as a shiver of attraction ran through her at Patrick's touch. He was the man who had everything, she reflected, good looks, brains and a regard for others, but he came from a background of incredible privilege—an alien world from hers. And however much he protested that class didn't come into it, she had a feeling his father wouldn't approve of his son forming an alliance with someone like her.

She looked up into his eyes, and felt herself beginning to melt. Still, Patrick was a big boy now, well able to stand up to his father. Was she ready to start up their fledgling relationship again, something that had never really got off the ground—or was that old demon stopping her, the demon that had always anticipated that something might go wrong ever since Terry had left her?

With a great effort she said briskly, 'I'm sorry, I've got to use these free days to do up the little cottage. I'm going to be taking stuff over and doing a bit of cleaning. Perhaps in a week or two…'

She allowed herself a bright little smile at him before she went to tell Max to collect the patient. Dammit, thought Patrick as he stared after her. He wasn't going to let it go. At the very least he had to mend bridges between them. It was sod's law that he should find Jandy even more desirable now, he pondered wryly.

It was an Indian summer's day, the warm sun filling the little front room of the cottage with light. Jandy ran up the stairs and went into the main bedroom armed with sweeping brushes, buckets and cloths, determined to clean the rooms up a bit before starting on the decorating. It all smelled a little musty so she opened a window, letting in the clean fresh air from outside, and swept dead flies and dust from the window sill before gazing out at the view beyond the pretty little garden.

She could see the beautiful mansion, Easterleigh House, where Patrick lived with his father, set on a slight hill through the trees. It looked magnificent from where she was, but very large—extraordinary to think that just three people occupied it! She supposed that the little house she'd leased was the former gatehouse for the estate. She thought she'd rather live in her cosy place than float around in that huge pad. She pulled a bucket towards her and got down on all fours to start scrubbing the floor.

Had she been wrong about refusing to see Patrick? Her thoughts inevitably drifted into thinking about him as she got into the rhythm of swirling the brush in the water and then going backwards and forwards over the wood. Perhaps she should have given him the chance to make amends after all, and she had missed an opportunity to build bridges.

She leant back on her heels for a second then shrugged. No, if he couldn't reveal these mysterious issues that made him wary of commitment, she'd done the right thing in keeping him at a distance. She went back to cleaning the floor with renewed vigour.

The sound of the front door banging shut made her start. She was quite sure she'd closed it before she'd come upstairs. She held her breath, wondering if it was an intruder, and her heart began to thump uncomfortably as she heard footsteps clumping their way up the stairs.

'Anyone there?' called a deep voice from the landing. Then the footsteps clattered on the wooden floor and Patrick appeared in the doorway dressed in faded jeans and an old white shirt, open at the neck. Her breath caught in her throat. He looked gorgeous! The casual look seemed to emphasise his broad shoulders and his tight, lean body. It wasn't fair, him appearing so suddenly, taking her off guard with no time to control the mixture of excitement and fizzing attraction that bolted through her body, making her stomach feel as if it had just looped the loop.

Jandy drew a deep breath and glared at him. 'For goodness' sake,' she said crossly. 'You gave me a hell of a fright... What are you doing here?'

'Sorry.' He grinned. 'I came on the off chance you'd be here. I thought you might be hungry. I've brought some food with me.'

But she wasn't going to give in to the leap of delight she'd had when he'd appeared, she told herself stubbornly. She was going to keep a tight rein on her emotions and play it very cool from now on. Caution told her that it would be better not to get too close to him.

'I'm very busy,' she said primly. 'I haven't time for food...'

'Of course you have,' he said firmly. 'It's a lovely day— we can eat outside. It might be the last really warm day we have before autumn. If you won't join me I'll have to eat alone.'

'I've a lot to do,' she said, waving her hand vaguely towards the walls.

'Oh, come on! It will give me a chance to make up for my churlishness the other day. Please....'

He looked at her wistfully, and suddenly Jandy wanted to laugh at the little-boy-lost expression on his face. Perhaps she should accept his olive branch.

She shrugged. 'It will have to be very quick, then.'

He had laid out a rug under an old apple tree near the

house, looking across the newly tilled fields. The sun still had warmth, and there was the slightest of breezes. Jandy sat down and clasped her hands round her knees, looking up at the white fluffy clouds sailing slowly across the sky. Was she a complete idiot, allowing herself to be alone with Patrick once again? She felt a tremor of excitement ripple through her, half hoping, half afraid, of what might happen in the intimate confines of the little garden.

She forced herself to relax and leant back against the apple tree, watching as Patrick opened a picnic basket to reveal a delicious feast. Then he uncorked a wine bottle and poured some sparkling wine into two plastic cups.

'The best you can get from Delford's supermarket,' he said solemnly. He held her eyes with his for a second. 'Cheers! Here's to us!'

Jandy sipped the wine rather self-consciously and was silent—she wasn't going to make the running. Looking across at him, his open shirt revealing a sexy muscled torso with dark hairs bristling through the top, and leaning casually on one elbow on the grass, she was afraid that she was ready to forgive him anything! If only he wasn't quite so devastating looking, or quite so physically close. If only his blue eyes weren't quite so beguiling… She lowered her gaze and concentrated on a beetle crawling across the grass. The atmosphere between them was electric.

He rocked back on his heels and looked at her assessingly, as if wondering how she was going to react to what he had to say.

'You need an explanation for my churlishness the other week,' he began slowly. 'As soon as I left you I was desperately sorry I'd hurt you.' He swirled the wine round in his glass for a second, before smiling ruefully at her. 'The fact is that when you told me what you'd been through, it made me realise that the last person you need in your life now is someone with problems of their own. You've got a measure of stability in your life now with little Abigail. I felt that I should keep at a distance before anything happened to threaten that.'

'Before what happened?' she queried impassively.

'You know what I mean, Jandy. In case we got too...close.'

Jandy stared at him warily, hearing her heart thump uncomfortably in her ears and trying to ignore the sexy aura he exuded so close to her.

'There was no need to be so rude,' she said as coolly as she could, while every fibre in her body longed to cuddle up to him, feel his arms around her.

He nodded and picked at the grass by his legs. 'I know—you're right. No excuse for it. But my reasons were valid enough.' He leaned towards her, a piece of dark hair flopping over his forehead, his blue eyes looking into hers. 'The thing is, Jandy, you know I have another very different life beyond the hospital and it's hard to reconcile the two.' He reached over and took her hand in his. 'But I want us to be friends—good friends. How can we work together if we're not?'

'I hope we can be that,' she said primly, his firm grip making her hand tingle. She felt the flutter of excitement in her tummy as the atmosphere almost pulsated with the tension between them. Her good intentions to play it cool seemed to be dissolving rather quickly.

Jandy attempted to pull her hands away from his, but he didn't allow that and held them even more firmly. 'I was frightened we were getting too close too quickly,' he admitted.

'For goodness' sake, we've only known each other for a few weeks,' she said lightly. 'I don't think that's a basis for lifelong devotion anyway.'

He gave a faint smile. 'The fact is, Jandy, I can't stop thinking about you—can't get you out of my head.' He stroked her cheek gently. 'You're always somewhere in my mind…'

She couldn't tear her eyes away from his penetrating blue gaze, wondering if she was hearing him properly, actually admitting that he did indeed feel something for her! He was facing her, so very close. She could see the little bit of stubble on his chin he'd missed while shaving, and the pulse beating in his neck. Excitement crackled through her body like little electric shocks.

She became very still, hardly breathing, as he gently brushed her hair back from her forehead.

'I think…know…that you weren't all that averse to me either,' he murmured.

Jandy averted her gaze, trying not to be seduced by those eyes, to ignore the thousand butterflies fluttering inside her.

She swallowed hard. 'And yet you want to keep me at a distance. Is this a warning?'

He swirled the wine round in his glass and watched the bubbles rising to the surface. 'It's complicated,' he said at last. 'You know about some of the things that occupy me outside work—my father's health and the issues regarding the house.'

'Yes, I can see that it's not easy.'

He grinned wryly at her. 'I guess I realised soon after I met you that there was a definite spark between us—quite a crackle actually.'

A little smile quirked Jandy's mouth—she would have described it as fireworks herself! She didn't say anything, but a little thrill of pleasure went through her that Patrick had actually admitted that he felt something for her too.

'Then I heard how you'd been treated by your boy-friend, and how you'd had to come to terms with his betrayal,' Patrick continued. 'Getting involved with someone like me—someone with a lot of baggage in their background—might jeopardise the stability you have now.'

Her brown eyes sparked at him. 'So what you want is a brief fling, is it? Not to be tied down. Sounds as if you want the best of all worlds,' she remarked crisply, unable to keep the sarcasm out of her voice.

He smiled sheepishly. 'It sounds like that—but I don't mean it to. Hell, I want us to be good friends and colleagues.' He tilted her face to his so that she couldn't avoid looking into his eyes. 'Or even more than that,' he said softly. 'But I want you to be aware of my situation.'

At least he was warning her—something Terry never had. And if she told him to get lost, he would probably do as she said. She felt her resolve weakening by the second and sighed, tossing back the wine in her glass. Then a feeling of bravado swept over her. Hadn't she been longing for some excitement in her life, to escape from the mundane everyday existence she led? He'd admitted that he was only ready for a fling, not a ring, but Patrick Sinclair was the first person since Terry to inject some passion and feeling into her soul.

She looked at the broad band of gold on his finger—a constant reminder of the wife he'd lost, she thought wistfully. Perhaps he'd never replace it, never be able to erase

Rachel's memory. But if he was up for a fling, then so was she—going into it with her eyes wide open, and to hell with memories and broken hearts!

'I don't mind being friends.' She tilted her chin almost defiantly. 'I may regret this, but honestly I'm sick of thinking back to what might have been, and what Abigail has missed not having Terry on hand. I want to look forward.'

He smiled down at her with those wonderful clear blue eyes and hugged her to him. 'You're a feisty girl, Jandy. Let's get to know each other a little better, then.'

He bent his head to hers and very gently brushed her lips lightly with his. And she knew this was the prelude to something much more momentous. She knew what was going to happen, and she did nothing to stop him. He drew back slightly, looking down at her.

'So can we be *very* good friends, do you think?' There was laughter dancing in his eyes as he asked her.

She didn't answer, but lifted her face to his, feeling again the tingle of his mouth against hers, and every nerve end in her body told her she needed more than that brief kiss. How could she ignore the great waves of longing flickering like butterflies inside her, her heart thumping with excitement against her ribs? Surely she was due a little affection, some fun, some excitement? But in a feeble effort to seem less eager she put her finger against his mouth for a second.

'Do you think this is wise?' she whispered.

He looked down at her. 'Let's not be wise all the time,' he said. 'Good friends are allowed to express their affection, aren't they?'

He kissed her again, this time harder, teasing her lips

open slightly, running his hand gently over her soft body, and she trembled because it was unbearably wonderful.

She wound her arms around his neck and pulled him towards her, opening her mouth to his and savouring the salty taste of him, feeling his body heavy and hard against hers as she fell back on the grass and he lay on top of her. The smell of the warm earth underneath them would always remind her of this moment. His mouth moved down her jaw with little butterfly kisses, and her body responded like a switch being flicked, pulling him close to her. He stopped for a second and looked down at her, his eyes twinkling.

'Is that a "yes" to my question, then?' he teased.

'I think so,' she whispered.

Perhaps she was jeopardising her future with a man who'd admitted he wasn't ready for a committed relationship, but at this particular moment she couldn't give a damn, she told herself as Patrick's hands moved over her body, gently touching her breasts, starting to undo her shirt. She wasn't even thinking how far they were going to go, she was revelling in his touch now, in the words he was murmuring in her ear. It was the present that mattered—the unbelievable sweetness of his firm, demanding frame on hers and the way her body reacted. It had been so long since she'd been held like this, or even wanted to be in anyone's arms, and the long-forgotten sensation of being made love to by someone she desired very much flooded over her. She was hungry for his kisses and more. And she knew that he was as eager as she was!

When the jarring sound of her mobile went off, Jandy couldn't think for a second what it was, except that it was intrusive and annoying. Then the stupid pop-song ringtone repeated itself again and again until reluctantly she pushed herself away from Patrick.

'Sorry,' she groaned. 'I'll have to get that—it could be about Abigail.'

Patrick rolled away and sighed. 'And we were just getting to know each other…' he murmured, looking across at Jandy and drawing one finger down her cheek.

She grabbed the phone and flipped it open, then Patrick watched her eyes widen in shock and her face pale slightly. He raised himself up on his elbow, concern crossing his face as she sat bolt upright, holding her mobile so tightly her knuckles were white.

'Lydia? Oh, my God….' she whispered. 'What's happened to her? Where is she?' She listened to the reply then seemed to gather herself together and said firmly, 'It's all right, darling—I'll go up. I've got a few days off anyway. You can't possibly get there as soon as I can. I'll organise things from this end.'

She snapped the mobile shut and turned to look bleakly at Patrick's questioning face. 'Is it your daughter?' he asked.

Jandy shook her head in a dazed way. 'No, not Abigail, thank God. It's my mother. She and her boyfriend, Bertie, have been involved in an accident. It was Lydia, my sister, on the phone, and she says it's serious.' She bit her lip, trying to keep her composure. 'Oh, Patrick, my mother's been through so much, and just when it seems she's at last found happiness, it could all be taken away from her. Bertie's in a bad way. As I told you, they live in Scotland—right up in the north—and I need to go to her as soon as I can.'

CHAPTER SEVEN

PATRICK took her hand and squeezed it, looking at her in concern. 'Do you know what kind of accident it was—a car crash, something at home?'

'My sister said that they were caught in a landslide on a mountainous road near where they live. Apparently they were lying trapped for over twelve hours. Both of them have multiple injuries.' She looked in a stunned sort of way at Patrick, large tears welling up in her eyes. 'I've got to get up there. My sister's on a long-haul flight to Australia and can't make it quickly.' She brushed the tears impatiently from her eyes. 'Dammit, I feel so helpless here.'

'Who will look after Abigail?' he asked.

'I'm sure Pippa, my childminder, will do that, and Abigail loves staying with her.' Jandy punched some numbers into her phone. 'I'll ring her now—and then I suppose I've got to get a flight to Inverness, it'll be far too slow to drive up there. Oh, Lord, there's so much to do...'

Patrick put his hand over hers and said firmly, 'You speak to Pippa. Meanwhile I'll get you a flight.'

She hadn't time to say how grateful she was to him. She

just nodded numbly and then spoke to Pippa, while Patrick walked away and contacted an airline on his mobile.

'That's it—all done,' he said briskly after a few minutes, putting his mobile back in his pocket. 'Our flight goes at five o'clock from Manchester.'

Jandy looked at him, slightly puzzled. '*Our* flight? Surely you've just booked one seat?'

He smiled, his eyes dancing rather wickedly. 'I'm coming with you,' he explained. 'And don't try and stop me!'

Jandy looked at him, completely dumbfounded, then she stammered, 'B-but why? You've got your own child to think about.'

'We've both got a few days off and, like you, I have someone perfectly competent to look after Livy. I can drive you round, act as a general dogsbody, while you see to your mother. Any objections?'

'I…I don't know… It's a lot to ask.' She shook her head tiredly. 'I don't like to put you to all this trouble.'

'It's no trouble,' he said firmly. 'You go home and organise your clothes and whatever you have to do for Abigail. I'll pick you up at about two o'clock.'

'But you can't drop everything for me. After all, we hardly—'

He held her arms and forced her to look at him. 'Know each other?' he finished with amusement. 'I guess we demonstrated a few minutes ago that we're reasonably good friends. And wasn't that what we said we were going to be? And as a good friend I'd like to help you—so relax and accept the offer!'

She felt too dazed to argue. 'Well…thank you,' she said weakly.

'Now, go on,' he urged. 'Pack what you need, and sort out Abigail. I'll see you soon.'

And all afternoon Jandy could hardly think of anything else except her mother, wondering just how badly she was hurt, what injuries she'd sustained. She felt like she was on autopilot, packing things for herself and Abigail without hardly taking in what she was doing. The flight to Inverness was a blur as Patrick found their seats, retrieved her luggage when they arrived and picked up the hire car to take them to the hospital. What would she have done without him?

Jandy and Patrick were shown immediately to the room in the hospital where her mother was. Jandy stood for a moment in the corridor, gathering the courage to go in. She was used to hospitals, wasn't she? It was no big deal being in one. Why, then, were her legs like jelly, her mouth so dry? Because she was at the receiving end of the bad news, she thought wryly. Seeing a hospital from a completely different point of view, knowing everything that could go wrong. She clutched Patrick's arm for a second.

'Patrick, I'm frightened—frightened of what I'm going to see. And I'm a nurse, for God's sake…'

'There's no shame in that, Jandy,' he said gently.

The nurse who'd taken her to the room smiled encouragingly at her. 'Mr Landers, the consultant, will see you after you've seen your mother. He'll explain everything to you—he's very able,' she assured Jandy.

'You go in,' urged Patrick. 'I'll go and get some basics like milk and bread while you're with her. She doesn't want someone she's never met barging in to see her.'

Leony Marshall was sitting propped up in the bed with

her eyes closed and a collar round her neck. Her whole face was bruised and swollen, her eyes puffy slits, and there was a gash across her forehead with a line of staples holding it together. Her right leg was slightly elevated and in a cast.

Jandy gave a sharp intake of breath at her mother's appearance, and swallowed hard. Her beautiful mother was almost unrecognisable, but bursting into tears wasn't going to help.

'Hello, Mum,' she whispered, laying a hand on her mother's arm and bending forward to kiss her gently on her cheek.

Her mother opened her eyes and an expression of amazement crossed her face as she saw her daughter. 'Jandy, darling!' she whispered through her stiff, swollen lips, 'I can't believe it—how wonderful it is to see you! How did you know I was here?'

'Lydia phoned me on a flight to Australia! The guy who helps Bertie at the garage managed to get in touch with her.'

Jandy took her mother's hand and Mrs Marshall squeezed it, mumbling, 'I'm afraid your old mum's a bit of a wreck at the moment…not looking my best!'

'Poor Mum. You must feel dreadful.'

'I'd feel better if you could find a cigarette for me— they've taken all mine away, the mean things!'

Jandy patted her mother's hand, feeling relief that her mother hadn't lost her spark or that mischievous sense of humour.

'You know there's no chance of that, Mum.' She smiled. 'The main thing is that these wounds will heal, and you'll be back to your beautiful self again. How did it happen?'

Leony looked woefully at her daughter. 'Bertie and I…we were driving into the hills to have a drink at a lovely little inn up there. It was so beautiful on the way that we stopped to take a photograph of the view at a lookout point halfway up.' She faltered, reliving the scene for a moment, then continued in a whisper, 'Suddenly there was the most tremendous roar and before we could turn round all these rocks and mud rained down on top of us—we had no time to get out of the way. It was terrible, darling. We were pinned underneath for hours.'

Jandy shook her head in disbelief. 'You could have been killed. Thank God you're still with us. What about Bertie?'

'They tell me he's got a skull fracture—he's been in Intensive Care.' Leony brushed aside a tear that slid down her swollen cheek. 'If anything happened to him, I don't know what I'd do, Jandy…he's been so good to me.'

'Now, don't get upset,' said Jandy soothingly. 'I'm going to speak to your consultant and find out exactly what they're doing for you and Bertie.' She eyed her mother's leg. 'You've obviously got a fracture—do you know where it's broken?'

'I think it's two breaks,' said her mother vaguely. 'The doctor called it something, but it meant nothing to me— you'd know what he meant, I'm sure.' She smiled weakly through stiff, painful lips. 'Oh, I can't tell you how glad I am you're here. I feel better already! But who's looking after little Abigail?'

'Oh. she's fine—Pippa's looking after her for as long as need be.'

'And what about your work? It must have been so difficult having to arrange everything, and get yourself to the airport.'

Jandy smiled. 'It wasn't as difficult as all that, Mum. I'm

off for a few days anyway, and er...a colleague did all the organisation of getting the tickets, coming over with me and driving me to the hospital.'

'How very kind—and how nice that you aren't alone... You must stay at the house, of course. There are clean sheets and towels in the cupboard, but it's a bit small for two of you. Pity there's only one usable room upstairs— you can use the sofa bed in the sitting room as the spare.'

'Don't worry, Mum, we'll manage!' Jandy's heart flipped slightly. She'd forgotten about the sleeping arrangements in the house. Just what would Patrick be expecting?

'And where is your colleague now?'

'Just getting some shopping,' said Jandy briefly. She wasn't quite ready to spring on her mother that her colleague was male and drop-dead gorgeous!

'Ah!' said a brisk voice from the door. 'I believe you're Mrs Marshall's daughter?'

Jandy turned round to see a tall bespectacled man standing in the doorway. The man held out his hand and shook hers vigorously.

'Yes,' she said with a smile. 'I'm Jandy Marshall.'

He nodded. 'You're very like your mother, I have to say. My name's Mr Landers and my team and I have been looking after Mrs Marshall since she was brought in.' He motioned to a chair by the bed. 'Please sit down and I'll explain the nature of your mother's injuries. You are a nurse, I believe? Then you'll understand when I explain that your mother has a Pott's fracture of her leg. Not very nice.'

Jandy grimaced. 'Poor Mum! So the fibula and tibia are both broken?'

He nodded. 'The fibula is broken just above the ankle

and the tibia's also fractured, resulting in dislocation. I've had to insert metal screws to hold the bone fragments in place.' Then he grinned. 'But don't worry! Your mother will eventually be back wearing the very high heels she was wearing when she was rescued!'

Trust her mother to be wearing high heels on a trip up a mountainside, thought Jandy. Not that she would have contemplated going for a walk when they'd reached the lookout spot—it would have been a cigarette stop!

'I shall hold you to that promise, Mr Landers,' whispered Leony from the bed. 'I wish you'd let me have just one teeny cigarette, though—it would be so good for my nerves!'

'Certainly not, Mrs Marshall,' he growled mock-severely. 'I want you to eat good food and perhaps have the odd glass of wine—but not one cigarette!' He turned to Jandy. 'The contusions on your mother's face look bad, but they're relatively minor and she's had a scan which shows that there's no bleeding or broken facial bones.'

'And how is Bertie, Doctor? Is he still in Intensive Care?' asked Jandy.

The doctor's expression turned more serious. 'Mr Muir is the neurosurgeon looking after your friend but he's in Theatre at the moment. He's asked me to tell you that Bertie has an open skull fracture with some inter-cranial bleeding—that's why he's in the Intensive Care department.'

'What does that mean?' asked Jandy's mother help-lessly. 'Oh, I'm so stupid. I don't even know what "cranial" means…'

'It means that there could be a build-up of blood around the skull and into the brain,' explained Jandy. 'Will they be doing anything to alleviate that?'

'Mr Muir intends to do a craniotomy to drain the blood and repair any damaged blood vessels.' He looked at Leony's horrified face, and put his hand up soothingly. 'There is every possibility that he will be all right—it is serious, yes, but not desperate. His condition is stable at the moment and we feel he can be operated on soon. I assure you that the patient will be in very good hands.'

'You'll tell me if…if his condition changes, won't you, Doctor?' asked Leony.

'Of course…but I want you to rest now, Mrs Marshall, and build up your strength. Sleep is a great healer.'

Leony sighed and said huskily, 'I shall never, never be able to sleep while my precious Bertie is in such danger.'

'Mr Landers is right, Mum,' said Jandy firmly. 'Bertie's obviously being closely monitored and you must try not to worry. I'll come back early tomorrow—but I'll be at the end of the phone if I'm needed.'

'Of course, darling—you must be shattered yourself.' Her mother brightened a little. 'Perhaps you'll bring me some better nighties than this awful hospital one and some face cream—and a little toilet water to freshen me up.'

Mr Landers's twinkling eyes met Jandy's. 'I think your mother feels a little better!'

'Of course, Mum. I should have thought of them myself, but I came straight here.' Jandy bent down to kiss her mother. 'I'll keep my fingers crossed for Bertie—but it sounds like he's having the best of attention. Would it be possible to see him soon?'

'At the moment he's sedated,' said Mr Landers. 'But I think tomorrow we'll see the picture more clearly and I'm sure you'll be able to see him then.'

Jandy went back to the car park relieved that her mother was not in danger but worried about the long-term arrangements for both Leony's and Bertie's convalescent care.

Patrick was standing by the hire car and waved to her. 'How are things?' he asked.

Jandy gave him a quick résumé of the situation then rubbed her eyes wearily. 'Lord, I feel like I've run a marathon,' she remarked with a sigh. 'Let's go to Mum's house—it's a good half hour away from here and up in the hills. I could do with a shower.'

'And something to eat?' put in Patrick with a grin. 'We never did get round to my picnic earlier today.'

'Was it only a few hours ago?' said Jandy in wonder. 'It seems a lifetime since we were in the garden...'

She caught his eye and blushed with a sudden giggle, remembering just what they had been doing when they'd been interrupted.

'We were getting to know each other quite well, weren't we?' Patrick murmured as he held the car door open for her. 'Now, get in and tell me the way to get to your mother's house.'

Jandy relaxed back against the car seat—she felt desperately tired, but the tension of the past few hours had disappeared. She flicked a look across at Patrick, concentrating on driving on the narrow country roads. It was incredibly comforting to have him with her, taking the burden off her shoulders of driving her to different places, and knowing he was there to unload her worries and discuss them with him.

Patrick felt her eyes on him. 'You worried about my driving?' He grinned.

'Not at all. I…I just want you to know how grateful I am, Patrick, you coming with me. It's a great help.'

'It's no hardship, Jandy. It's a beautiful area, and if it weren't for your mother's terrible accident I could imagine we were on holiday. It's been too long since I've had a few days to myself.' He glanced at her mischievously. 'And with a beautiful woman I intend to get to know very, very well. And don't forget we've some unfinished business to complete…'

Jandy laughed, suddenly feeling light-hearted after the strain of the past hours. The circumstances that had brought her up to Scotland were awful, but there was definitely a silver lining to the cloud. Her heart skipped a beat—alone with the sexiest man she'd ever seen! A tremor of nervous excitement ran through her. Being thrown together with a man she didn't really know for a few days could make or break a friendship. And everything seemed to have happened so quickly. Only a short while ago she'd been furious with him and his supposed snobbery, and now, only that morning, a few hours ago, he'd apologised for his rudeness and made it very clear that the attraction she felt wasn't all one-sided! She flicked a look at his strong profile—she didn't know what would happen between them over the next few days, but one thing was for sure, she fancied him even more than ever!

Lost in her thoughts, she nearly missed the crossroads where the little filling station stood at the side of the road, overlooking the valley they just driven from.

'We're here, Patrick—this is it!' she sang out.

Patrick drew into the drive and got out, stretching his long limbs and looking around him. 'Wow! This is a little piece of paradise,' he murmured. 'What a backdrop. It…it doesn't seem real, more like a scene from a romantic film.'

They were fairly high up in the hills, the garage the last stop for petrol before motorists headed over the tops. Flower tubs filled with geraniums had been placed along the front and the garage was painted a fresh white, with a little coffee shop to one side. There was the faintest smell of honey permeating the still-warm air from the heather creeping across the moorland and right up to the garden of the house. Tumbling over the little walls that bounded a small terrace round the front of the property were fading morning glory blooms and more pink geraniums.

'Idyllic—what a lovely place. I've never seen a filling station like it!' Patrick remarked appreciatively, turning to look down across the countryside, where in the distance beyond was the sea, glinting and sparkling in the late afternoon sun.

'It's beautiful, isn't it?' Jandy said.

He looked at her silently for a moment, standing with her back to the dying sun, a slender silhouette, her hair highlighted a mellow honey gold in the light, little tendrils that had escaped from her chignon framing her face.

'Yes,' he said quietly. 'Quite beautiful.'

'But it's miles away from anywhere, or any help for that matter, so Mum and Bertie can't stay here until they're fit.' Jandy bit her lip, her forehead creased with worry. 'What on earth can we do? They have someone to help them with the garage and car servicing side—I'll have to have a word with him now before he goes.'

She went round to the garage where there was much hammering and a pair of legs protruding from under a jacked-up car.

'Ian?' she shouted. 'Can I have a word?'

A young man slid out from under the car, his face smeared liberally with black grease. He wiped his hands on a piece of rag and shook Jandy's hand.

'Och, I'm sorry about your mother and Bertie—it's a bad do!' he exclaimed. 'How are they?'

'Not so bad, Ian, but it's going to take some time for them to recover enough to get back to work.' Jandy introduced him to Patrick and then added, 'Do you think you can manage for a while by yourself? It would be awful to have to shut the place down.'

He grinned, teeth white against his oily face. 'No trouble, Jandy. I was wondering, though—would it be all right if I brought my girlfriend Netta to do the coffees and teas? She could do with the extra money and she'd be a help with the pumps too.'

'Sounds a great idea,' said Jandy, her spirits lifting slightly. 'And perhaps Netta might stay on for a bit while my mother and Bertie convalesce?'

'I think she'd be happy to do that,' agreed Ian.

'Let's talk about that later,' suggested Patrick, looking at Jandy's weary face. 'We'll sit out here while there's still some warmth in the air and have a glass of wine.' He put his hands on her shoulders and looked down at her. 'You need to unwind a bit after the shock you've had, and you've done all you can for one day.'

'Aye,' agreed Ian kindly. 'You get yourselves sorted. I'll see to the work out here. No need for you to worry yourselves. I'll be off soon, but I'll see you tomorrow.'

Jandy nodded. 'Thanks, Ian. I'm really grateful for your support.'

She went up the path towards the house and Patrick

followed with their luggage. She stood for a moment looking down the valley, trying to push the worries about her mother to the back of her mind. Tiredly she leant against Patrick for a second, drawing comfort from his physical presence. He wrapped his arms around her and pressed her to him so that she could feel the thud of his heart against hers.

'It's all right, sweetheart, relax...give yourself some time off from worrying.'

His voice rumbled over her head, calming, soothing. He looked down at her, locking his eyes with hers, and she felt that crackle of attraction flash between them. There was nothing to stop them doing anything they wanted, she thought. It should be so idyllic, alone together with the damp scent of a Highland evening drifting over to them— and yet she pulled back from him. How easy it would be to enjoy the moment and take up again where they'd started just that morning in the garden of the little house—make love with no inhibitions, just pure physical fulfilment. Wasn't that what she longed for?

But that had been that morning, and so much had happened since then and she'd had time to reflect on her impetuosity. There was this nagging thought that to her it would mean much more than it would to Patrick. Yes, she wanted him like crazy, but she needed stability too.

'What is it, Jandy?' he asked, sensing her reluctance and putting his hand under her chin to force her to look at him. He searched the expression on her face and smiled wryly. 'It's not the right time, is it? I'm not completely insensitive. If you think I'm going to take advantage of you in this heavenly place, however much I want to, I assure you I won't. I won't do anything you don't want me to. I respect you too much for that.'

Respect, thought Jandy bleakly. Hardly the most romantic thought. She needed love as well.

She drew back from him and wandered down the small garden, sitting on the little wall by the road. 'Tell you what—let's have that glass of wine.'

They didn't sit too near each other as they sipped their wine. It was almost as if they were playing a waiting game, incredibly conscious of each other. They'd crossed over some sort of threshold that morning and now Jandy felt suddenly self-conscious, unsure where the next move would take them. She took another large slurp of the crisp white wine and began to feel a little less stressed, the tensions of the day slipping away.

Patrick glanced across at Jandy. He could see her profile as she leant her head back against the wall, her eyes closed and the sweep of her eyelashes fanned against her cheek. He longed to touch her, take her in his arms and make love to her, but some inner instinct told him to take it slowly. Don't rush her, Patrick, he told himself. One step at a time.

After a few minutes he said softly, 'Tell me how your mother came to find this place.'

Jandy smiled. 'She's been a star really—bringing up the two of us by herself. Dad died when we were in our early teens. Mum worked in a little dress shop in Delford and did some of their buying for them. She was sent to look at some clothes in a small factory in Inverness—and she met Bertie when her car broke down. He was the mechanic who mended it. He's about twelve years younger than her, but they fell in love and have been together ever since! This was his little house.'

'What a romantic tale,' murmured Patrick. 'And do you like him?'

'He's a lovely guy—and he's made Mum so happy. Just the right man for her. The age difference doesn't seem to matter in the least.'

'If you find the right person, that sweeps all other considerations aside, doesn't it?'

Jandy looked at him wryly. 'I don't think your father would agree with that!'

Patrick got up and came over to her, sitting on the wall beside her and taking her hands, an amused expression on his face.

'You've got a thing about my father,' he said. 'He's not the dinosaur you think he is. The thing is, circumstances have made him wary about choosing a partner for life.'

'I'm with him there,' sighed Jandy.

'Like you, I lost a parent when I was young,' Patrick said. 'My mother died when I was three, and then my brother and I had a nanny, a lovely person. She's still alive, bless her.'

'I'm sorry about your mother,' murmured Jandy, reflecting what different experiences she and Patrick had had when they were children. There had been no such things as nannies for her sister and herself when they'd been young! Her mother had scraped a living and they had never been hungry or without a roof over their heads, but a childhood in a place like Easterleigh was a world away from the council estate she'd been brought up in.

'Actually, Robert and I had a very happy childhood— until my father remarried, that is.' Patrick's mouth tightened. 'She wasn't the best of step mothers, I'm afraid, and it wasn't a happy marriage.'

A sudden memory of Patrick's first day at work flicked into Jandy's mind—the little boy with the head injury, Jimmy Tate, and his cold, unsympathetic stepmother—and Patrick's reaction to that case.

'What did your stepmother do to you?' she asked quietly.

He shrugged. 'That's water under the bridge now—but she left me with this little legacy.' He turned his face to Jandy and pointed to the white raised scar down the side of his face. Her eyes widened in horror.

'She did that to you? What did she…?'

A wry smile touched his lips. 'Robert and I had been making a noise. She had no patience with children and had snapped at us to shut up, saying that we'd have no supper if we weren't quiet—her usual form of punishment. I had a temper and shouted that she was a wicked witch. She flung a pan at me and the the rim caught my face.'

'She could have killed you…'

'She was certainly frightened, because, like all facial wounds, it bled like crazy. But she said if I told anyone, she'd make life very difficult for my younger brother. And I knew she meant it—she could be cruel.'

Jandy reached out and took Patrick's hand. 'You poor little boys,' she whispered. 'You must have felt quite helpless.'

'I certainly know what cruelty does to a child,' he said grimly. 'Visible signs like my scar are one thing—the emotional scars are harder to see.'

Jandy looked into his eyes and stroked his face, her finger drawing a line down his jaw to his mouth, moving gently over the jagged white line.

'I was wrong, then.' She smiled. 'I thought it was a bad rugby tackle. How terrible for a young child to have to cope with that.'

'She left my father when he became disabled and too frail to stand up to her,' said Patrick simply. 'It was a particularly unpleasant time, and she took him for every penny she could. That's partly why my father is so eager to start the wind-farm business.'

'And you came back to help him. Is your brother involved as well?'

'No. He has nothing to do with the project,' he said wryly. 'Robert still lives in London, leading a merry bachelor life.'

They both sat in silence for a moment, gazing out over the tree-lined valley, and then there was the unmistakeable growl of thunder in the distance. Patrick looked up at the sky, which had darkened considerably. Black clouds were rolling over the mountains and there were flickers of lightning over the hills. A few large drops of rain began to fall, and he stood up and pulled Jandy to her feet.

'There's a storm brewing. Let's go in and have some of this food I've bought.'

They gathered up their shopping and cases, but before they could reach the front door a flash of lightning and an enormous crack of thunder exploded almost over their heads. Quite suddenly a deluge of rain was pouring over them, pelting down like a waterfall, the drops leaping off the path as soon as they hit the ground. The temperature already seemed to have dropped several degrees.

Jandy fumbled with the keys and by the time she'd opened the door, they were both completely drenched. She slammed the door shut and they looked at each other then both began laughing helplessly. They were soaked to the skin, their hair plastered against their heads, water running in rivulets down their clothes, forming puddles on the floor.

'What are we like?' she spluttered through gales of laughter. 'We might just as well have been swimming in our clothes!'

Their laughter died down and they stared at each other silently for a few seconds. Then Patrick's blue eyes darkened and he put his hand under her chin, tilting her face to his. She didn't put up a fight when he pulled her towards him. At the back of her mind she knew that what was going to happen was inevitable. So Patrick couldn't offer long-term commitment? It was too late to worry about that now. The sudden rainstorm had made them both relax, and the wine had taken the edge off her feeble resolve.

'What a beautiful waterlogged mermaid you are,' he murmured huskily. Then he kissed her hungrily, his lips moving down her neck to the little hollow in her throat, his hands running lightly over her soft curves and making her arch against his muscled body.

'Don't you think we ought to take these clothes off?' he murmured. 'My nanny always said it was bad for you to stay in wet things…'

She laughed at him through the damp tendrils of hair dripping over her face. 'Did you always do what your nanny told you?' she asked mock-primly, again weakly attempting to put the brakes on the fiery physical attraction that was crackling between them.

He looked at her solemnly. 'It was more than my life was worth to disobey her, sweetheart.'

And suddenly they were both tearing their clothes off, leaving them where they lay on the floor. All Jandy could concentrate on were Patrick's arms twined around her and their naked bodies pressed against each other, slippery from their damp clothes. Too late to call a halt now, she thought hazily—and neither did she want to.

He whispered throatily, 'I can't tell you how often I've longed to do this over the past few weeks, my darling. You are so beautiful...'

He held her away from him for a second, his eyes feasting on her slender curves, the soft fullness of her breasts. Then he trailed his fingers delicately down her stomach, and covered her with butterfly kisses, and every nerve in Jandy's body responded as his lips drew a path of fire down her body. He pulled her down onto the floor, and she didn't resist as his hands brought her to a pitch of excitement. This was what she had missed for so long, and even if Patrick had said he was not a long-term prospect, for the time being he was hers—and the memory of her betrayal by Terry began to fade.

CHAPTER EIGHT

GRADUALLY Jandy woke from a deep sleep and opened her eyes then stared around the room, disorientated for a few seconds by the unfamiliar surroundings. Then everything that had happened the night before came flooding back to her, and a little smile of contentment curved across her face as she stretched languorously under the quilt.

It had been the most amazing night of her life, she thought happily. Of course, the night her darling Abigail had been born had been wonderful too, holding that miraculous little bundle in her arms—but it had been mixed with bitter-sweet memories. She'd adored her baby as soon as she'd held her in her arms—but there'd been no father there to welcome his child into the world, no champagne or flowers from a husband or lover, but the very real worry about how she was going to support her new baby. Lying in her hospital bed and seeing the other mothers with their doting partners had been hard to bear.

But last night had been unadulterated ecstasy, when two people had given absolutely to each other. She had no regrets, even though Patrick had put his cards on the table.

He had said he wasn't up for a long-term relationship, but after last night she was convinced that they had a future together. How could anyone make love like he had and not feel more than a passing regard for her?

Light-heartedly she swung her legs over the bed and padded over to the window. The day was a complete contrast to the night before, with bright sunshine gleaming on the rain-washed road. In the distance the mountains were navy blue against the duck-egg blue of the skies and everything looked fresh and reinvigorated. Like she felt, said Jandy to herself, with a little thrill of happiness.

'Can I come in?' said a deep voice.

'No. I've nothing on yet,' replied Jandy sternly, trying not to giggle.

'Good—that's how I like you!'

Patrick shoved the door open with his elbow and entered the room carrying a tray laden with tea and toast. He put it down on a chair and came towards her with a happy smile on his face.

'You look delectable, my sweet,' he said softly, gathering her in his arms and kissing her extravagantly.

Jandy made a half-hearted attempt to push him away. 'Patrick! This isn't the time…'

He looked at her with wide, innocent eyes. 'Oh? Why not?'

She laughed. 'As your nanny might have said—because! Anyway, I want to get to the hospital early and I've got to have a shower.'

'Oh…that!' he said absently, and continued to kiss her until they both fell in a heap on the bed. And Jandy didn't say anything more for some time…

Afterwards Patrick said tenderly, stroking back her honeyed hair from her face, 'You're wonderful, my sweet. I'll never, never forget this day, forget you—even when I'm old and grey…'

Then they lay in each other's arms for a while, until the front door rang and Jandy was galvanised into action, wriggling out from under Patrick and scurrying for a jacket to put on.

'Oh, no, Patrick, that's probably Ian! And we've got to get to the hospital. I'm not ready and neither are you!'

'It won't take me long. You have that tea and toast I brought and a quick shower, and then we'll be off. I'll answer the door. I'm the only one who should look at you when you're totally naked—I'm selfish that way!'

Jandy giggled and threw a pillow after him as he went out of the room. As long as her mother and Bertie were going to be OK, the future suddenly looked bright and exciting. She knew she had fallen hook, line and sinker for Patrick, and she was sure he felt the same way about her.

'Have you been to see Bertie yet?' asked Leony from her hospital bed, anxiously looking at Jandy. 'Nobody will tell me anything about his state of health. Please go and see him if you can.'

'I will, Mum—don't worry. I'm going to see his consultant when he's done his rounds.'

'Thank you, darling.' Mrs Marshall looked at her daughter appraisingly. 'You do look well—quite blooming! You must have had a good night's sleep last night after all your travelling yesterday!'

'Very good indeed,' replied Jandy, unable to stop a broad

grin spreading over her face. Not surprising after the energetic episode before it!

'And you managed to put up the sofa bed for your colleague OK?'

'Er…yes, no trouble there,' said Jandy, adding quickly, 'How do you feel today, Mum? I think you definitely look brighter and the swelling on your face seems to have subsided.'

'I'm on the mend, feeling better today. In fact, they say as soon as I've found someone to look after me, I can go home as all I need is rest and to keep my foot off the ground.' She put her hand up quickly as she saw the concern on Jandy's face.

'I know that you've got to get back to Abigail and work but perhaps we could find someone from the village for a few weeks?'

'Ian suggested his girlfriend might help,' said Jandy.

'Netta? Oh, that would be lovely—she's a sweet girl. Do you think that could be organised, then?'

'Of course. I'm glad you know her—that makes it easier.'

Her mother smiled. 'What a relief it will be to go home! I must be getting better because I'm getting so bored now, although they've been wonderful to me in the hospital. What about bringing your colleague in? I'd love to meet her—so kind of her to come up with you. Is she a nurse too?'

Jandy hesitated for a second. Her mother was of a romantic turn of mind and would very quickly put two and two together when she met Patrick!

'Actually, it's a he and he's a doctor in A and E,' she said brightly.

144 FROM SINGLE MUM TO LADY

'Oh, I see! But that's wonderful!' exclaimed her mother, looking at her searchingly.

Jandy almost laughed, her mother's thoughts were so transparent! She was obviously already marrying her daughter off to this eligible man she'd never met!

'I'll go and get him, Mum. He's looking forward to meeting you too.'

It was obvious from the moment she saw him that Leony was bowled over by Patrick—and she observed accurately that her daughter was too!

'I'm so grateful to you for coming up with Jandy,' she said to him. 'It's lovely that she's got someone to look after her while she's up here.'

'I'm just glad I was able to be of some help,' said Patrick, adding with a grin, 'And you do live in a beautiful part of the world…'

'Then you must both come up for a proper holiday soon, and explore the whole area together,' said Leony. 'It would be lovely to get to know you better!'

'I think we'll go and see Bertie and find out how he is then we can report back to you,' said Jandy hastily, before her mother could start organising a wedding reception!

As they turned to go out, Leony took hold of Jandy's arm. 'Just one moment on your own, darling,' she said in a low voice. 'I won't keep her a minute, Patrick—you go on down to see Bertie.'

'What is it, Mum?' asked Jandy, looking at the frown on Leony's face.

'I…I couldn't help wondering. Patrick's wearing a wedding ring—does that mean he's married?'

'He's a widower, Mum…he's got a little girl.' She

smiled and patted her mother's hand. 'Don't worry, I'm not about to fall for another Terry!'

Her mother smiled and relaxed back against the pillows. 'You know it's just that I wouldn't want you to be hurt again—falling for a married man can only lead to trouble. Of course, if he's a widower...'

'See you later!' Jandy smiled, blowing her a kiss from the door. 'As I said—don't worry!'

But as she followed Patrick down the stairs to ICU she sighed. That wedding ring was a sign that he hadn't forgotten his wife—in a way, as long as he wore it, Rachel was still in the picture.

The ICU was quiet, just the dull thrum of machines and clicking of monitoring equipment keeping track of the condition of the patients in the unit. Bertie was sedated and had an oxygen mask over his face, and a nurse was busy checking his vital signs, fluid balance, blood oxygen levels and blood pressure. She turned and smiled at Jandy and Patrick.

'Bertie's had his craniotomy,' she said. 'He's doing very well, and breathing by himself. He's going to the high-dependency unit very soon, and after a day or two there he'll be going to the general ward. Mr Muir wants to have a word with you if you'll go to his office.'

'Phew—what a relief,' breathed Jandy to Patrick. 'I don't know how I could have told Mum if anything had gone wrong with Bertie's operation.'

Mr Muir had the look of an elderly chick, with fluffy grey hair standing up over his round head and a little beak nose, but when he spoke his voice was surprisingly loud—but reassuring and confident.

'We're very pleased indeed with Bertie's progress,' he boomed. 'He had an open skull fracture, which led to some cranial bleeding. But we've drained the blood and managed to repair some damaged blood vessels. With any luck, he should be as good as new soon.' He chuckled. 'Surprising how well the human body can restore itself after a major trauma, isn't it?'

'Not without some intervention on your part,' said Jandy, smiling. 'We're so grateful to you, Mr Muir.'

'Not at all, not at all.' He smiled. 'He'll be kept in for a little while yet, just to be monitored, but we don't antici-pate any complications. You can tell your mother that her friend will be as good as new soon!'

Leony had been allowed home after Netta had promised to come in every day, and stay the night if need be, when Jandy and Patrick had returned to Delford. Leony sat in a high-backed chair downstairs with a smile on her bruised face.

'I can't believe I've made it home—a few days ago I wouldn't have thought I'd be back for months!' She turned to Jandy. 'I know you've got to get back to Abigail, darling, but you've both been wonderful to give up everything and come and see me—I'm so grateful.'

'We're going back on the evening plane tonight, Mum. There isn't much room for Netta and us in the house together! I'm going to dash out now to get some shopping. Patrick's just gone for an exploratory walk but Ian's only across the way at the garage so if you need him, ring him on his mobile.'

'I'll be fine, Jandy. I'll sit and look out at the view— I've missed it all so much.'

* * *

Patrick whistled a low contented tune to himself as he strode along the woodland path. He loved this part of the world, the majestic mountains and the beautiful lochs. He and Jandy would come back soon with Abigail and Livy and have a proper holiday: he felt sure the little girls would be great companions for each other. Over the past few days he had felt the weight of sadness that had always seemed to accompany him begin to lift. Gradually he'd begun to realise that he couldn't imagine a future without Jandy. She was everything he needed—funny, sweet and very beautiful. A short time ago he'd told her he couldn't make a permanent commitment—how wrong he'd been! Now all he could think about was being with her for ever. He was a lucky man.

He flicked a look at his watch. It was time to get back— Jandy would have finished her shopping soon and then they could have lunch and make their way to the airport later on for the evening flight.

Their cases were already packed and he would load them into the car later. He went into the kitchen by the back door. Jandy was evidently back: he could hear her voice and Leony's chatting together. He put the kettle on to make coffee, and as he waited for it to boil their conversation floated across to him.

'Patrick's absolutely adorable, darling, I do like him,' he heard Leony say, as he poured the water onto the ground coffee in the percolator. 'He's so reliable and kind. And as for his looks…'

Patrick grinned. She was quite gushing sometimes, but very sincere and amusing—he liked Jandy's mother a lot. He went to the door to make some glib comment about her remarks. Jandy was standing with her back to him, her silky, honey-coloured hair brushing her shoulders, slender in cut-off jeans. Her voice floated clearly towards him through the door.

'I'm glad to hear you approve,' she was saying with a laugh. 'And, of course, the best thing is he's got to be so secure financially. Getting married to him would sure solve a lot of money problems. Unusual to find a guy who ticks all the right boxes and is rolling in money as well, isn't it?'

She said it in a carefree way—no mention of her being in love with him, just the fact that as a supposedly wealthy man he'd passed some sort of test. Patrick stood stock still, frozen with shock, at the door, wondering if he was hearing things—but, no, Jandy was adding to her remarks.

'Just think—"Lady Janet Sinclair" sounds pretty good, doesn't it?'

Patrick's throat constricted and he turned away, sick to his stomach. He gripped the side of the work top and bent his head, suddenly feeling nauseous and dizzy, utterly stunned by Jandy's remarks. His beautiful Jandy... He could hardly believe it—and yet he'd heard her, seen her. The bitter taste of bile rose in his mouth. Hadn't he been in this place before—someone who only wanted him for his wealth? Jandy, his beautiful, kind Jandy, he thought in bewilderment, had turned out to be nothing but a gold-digger.

An immense and overwhelming sadness flooded over him and he stared miserably out of the window. His life seemed littered with mistakes—the guilt he would always carry for his beloved Rachel's death, his foolishness in getting entangled with Tara. Only this time it was much,

much worse because he'd allowed himself to fall in love with Jandy, to imagine a future with her. His mouth tightened. He felt he'd been punched in the solar plexus as he'd realised that Jandy's attraction for him was founded on nothing more than the fact that she thought he was a wealthy man. Bitterly he reflected that it was a rerun of his relationship with Tara. There was no future for them if all she was interested in was his money—money, he thought wryly, that he didn't have.

A stab of fury went through him, sudden disgust at a woman he'd thought had liked him for himself alone. They could have had a marvellous future together, and he believed she would have been a wonderful mother to Livy—and Livy would have had a little companion. All that longed-for happiness seemed to have turned to dust and ashes in a few minutes.

His brain raced. One thing he couldn't bring himself to do was confront her on the matter at the moment, but he couldn't bear to sit next to her on a plane for an hour. God, only that morning they had made passionate love to each other. She'd been so warm and loving, and they had been everything to each other—he'd thought. But now, knowing what her real motives were… He closed his eyes and swallowed painfully at the thought of her betrayal.

He gazed out of the window without seeing the view then, as if making a sudden decision, he reached into his jacket for a pen and scribbled a note on the back of an envelope, sticking it on the fridge door. Then he took out his mobile and went into the back garden. He made a couple of phone calls, picked up his case and strode to the crossroads without looking back.

* * *

'Where's Patrick?' asked Jandy, appearing at the front door. Her arms were weighed down by two huge bags of shopping, which she dumped on the floor. Then she sat down by her mother.

'He's not back yet,' said Leony. 'I thought I heard him in the kitchen, but I must have been mistaken. Guess who turned up in a taxi just after you'd gone to the shops! Your sister. I'm so thrilled that she's managed to get a few days off! She's just gone to say hello to Ian, but I've been telling her all about Patrick.'

Jandy laughed. 'Honestly, Mum, there's nothing to tell. We've made no commitment to each other. He's got lots of problems that have to be sorted—we're just having a good time!'

'Of course, darling, but anyone can see he's besotted with you. And I don't think you're too averse to him either, are you?'

Of course she wasn't averse to him—she was absolutely wild about him, she was drunk with happiness whenever she saw him! The more she saw him, the more she wanted him, to be with him, to make love with him! Jandy got up quickly—she had to keep a level head. She mustn't presume too much about Patrick: she must let things take their time.

'I'll go and see Lydia,' she said happily. 'What a lovely surprise! She must have come straight up when she came back from her Australian flight.'

Just at that moment Lydia came through the door and the two sisters hugged each other ecstatically.

'It's so good to see you, Lydia.'

'I haven't got another long-haul flight for a week, so I

thought I'd come up and help look after Mum because I know you've got to get back to Abigail and work.'

'That's great. A load off my mind...'

Lydia pulled her down on the sofa 'Now, come on, sis, no secrets now! Mum's been telling me all about this super doc you've brought up with you! How's it going with you and him?'

'Mum and you are the biggest nosy parkers in the land,' declared Jandy. 'Look, let's make lunch before Patrick gets back from his walk and I'll tell you what there is to tell—not that there is much, I assure you! Help me take the shopping through.'

Jandy picked up a bag and went through to the kitchen, placing it on the table, and started taking things out of it to put in the fridge. Then she noticed an envelope, with writing scribbled across it, stuck on the fridge door. She picked it up and read it slowly, her eyes widening in disbelief and disappointment.

'Oh! I don't believe this! Patrick's had to go urgently to his father—he's managed to get an earlier flight via Glasgow. He got a taxi to take him to the airport.' She looked at Lydia, puzzled. 'You'd have thought he would have rung me on my mobile. His father must be very bad for him to take off like that—and I was dying for you to meet him.'

'And I was dying to give him the once-over,' said Lydia. 'How dare he go before I got the chance to see him? I'll just have to rely on Mum's glowing reports to see if he's suitable for my darling sister, although he sounds just right in every way!'

Jandy took out her mobile and punched in Patrick's number, but after a few rings she gave up. 'He's either turned it off or the reception's bad up here,' she sighed. 'I hope nothing drastic has happened.'

A little niggle of worry flickered in the back of her mind. It was such a very brief note—almost terse. And he hadn't signed it with 'love', she thought irrationally. Surely you'd do that to a woman you'd made passionate love to only that morning? Suddenly the day didn't seem so carefree after all.

CHAPTER NINE

'JUST get me some requisition sheets from that cupboard, will you?' asked Karen as she and Jandy straightened up one of the small cubicles and remade a bed with fresh linen and pillow cases. She looked at Jandy sympathetically as she took the papers from her. 'You've had a busy time up in Scotland, I believe. How's your poor mother after that ghastly accident?'

'She's making a great recovery. Her face looks better already, although her leg will be in a cast for a while. It was a pretty complicated fracture, but my sister's with her at the moment and there's someone who'll be coming in every day when Lydia has to start work again.'

'It was great that Patrick was able to go with you,' commented Karen, flicking an interested glance at Jandy as she started to look through her stock list. 'I should think he was a wonderful support.'

Karen wasn't a gossip but Jandy was shy about telling people that they were more than just good friends. It was early days yet, she thought. In fact, they'd only been properly 'together' for two days!

'Oh, he was. He suggested coming with me when he heard

that my mother and her partner had been injured. We both had a few days off and it certainly made everything much easier, having him to drive me about and do the shopping.'

Jandy didn't add that it had made what could have been a fraught situation one of the most romantic episodes in her life! She bit her lip thoughtfully. It was odd that she'd been back at work a day and still hadn't heard from Patrick. Although she'd phoned him once or twice without success, he'd never got back to her. She had an uneasy feeling that something awful had happened—perhaps so awful that he hadn't had time to contact her and tell her exactly why he'd had to leave Scotland so abruptly.

'Er...have you heard how his father is?' she asked Karen. 'Patrick had to leave in a rush—something about his father—but I haven't been able to find out what's happened. He's probably been too busy to let me know.'

Karen looked up from making notes on the stock list and shook her head. 'He hasn't mentioned anything about his father, but Patrick's on this shift anyway, so you'll be able to ask him. I do know he's requested a few days off for holiday from next week.'

Jandy felt a flash of disappointment. She had looked forward so much to seeing him again, and had assumed that he would be as anxious as her to grab a few minutes alone together and arrange an evening out. If he was going on holiday, there'd be very little opportunity to meet.

Bob popped his head into the cubicle. 'Four patients are due in from an RTA any minute. Can you be on standby, please? One very serious injury at least.'

Back to the grindstone, sighed Jandy, going with Tilly to make sure four cubicles were cleared and ready with drips and any other equipment that might be necessary. It all seemed a far cry from twenty-four hours ago and a romantic night filled with passion in the Highlands with Patrick, she reflected wryly.

Bob was making a rapid initial examination of the casualties who'd just been wheeled in—two elderly men and a youth were being held in the assessment area.

'What happened?' he asked the paramedic.

'They were coming out of a pub and standing near a taxi rank. A car came careering round a corner overtaking a bus and went out of control. These three copped it, I'm afraid, and the driver finished up against a wall. He'll be here in a minute when they've stabilised him—he's lucky to be alive.'

'Right… Ah, Patrick, here you are. Can you deal with the patient we've put in the clean theatre?'

Jandy looked round quickly when she heard Patrick's name, ready to smile at him and hold his gaze in a little secret intimacy, but he was striding towards Bob from the ambulance bay and he didn't seem to notice Jandy as he passed her. He listened closely to Bob as he ran through the patient's condition.

'This young man's eighteen and his name's Jed,' explained Bob. 'He's in a lot of pain and it seems to be around his thorax. Plus he's got facial and arm wounds with dirt and gravel in them that need attention. Staff, can you and Nurse Rodman clean those out?'

In the clean theatre where minor surgical procedures were performed under aseptic conditions, Jandy and Tilly began to cut away the patient's clothing then started to work methodically, using swabs and forceps to pick out the grit and other dirt from the wounds. Jandy was intensely aware of Patrick working close to her, also very conscious that he hadn't, even by a nod or a smile, acknowledged her presence. But, then, of course he was concentrating on his patient, just as he should be, she told herself sharply.

Patrick was murmuring to Jed, his voice low and reassuring: 'It's all right, Jed, you'll be fine. You're doing well. Don't worry, Jed, we'll be giving you something for that pain very soon.'

He used his patient's name often, trying to hold the young man's attention and keep him calm, realising that it was pain and shock that was causing the touch of hysteria in Jed's voice.

'I need to let my girlfriend know—I should be meeting her now...' he kept repeating, with a rising inflection. 'She won't know where I am. I've got to meet her, you see...'

'Where were you meeting her, Jed? Tell me, and someone will contact her, I promise,' Patrick said soothingly.

'Her name's Rachel and it's on my mobile in my pocket. She'll be worried if I don't turn up.'

'Sister will ring her for you. Get his mobile out of his trouser pocket, would you, Staff?'

Patrick moved his hands over the youth's rib cage, checking for any misalignment, watching Jed's face as he did so and not the area being felt so that he could tell immediately if he touched a cracked rib or a torn muscle.

Jed moaned and shifted his body from side to side restlessly, showing all the signs of acute discomfort, bending and straightening his legs. Occasionally he coughed, bringing up blood.

'What happened? What happened?' he mumbled. 'Something crashed into me...'

'It was a car, Jed—it took a corner too quickly. You were outside the pub,' Jandy said quietly, trying to help Jed orientate himself. 'You're in the hospital now and we're helping you.'

Patrick looked up from examining Jed, his eyes meeting Jandy's for a second, but oddly cold and remote. 'Staff, would you get Bob Thoms, please?'

His voice was authoritative, terse. It was as if he and Jandy had never had a relationship at all. There was no trace of softness in his expression, just stern preoccupation.

He was only being professional, Jandy told herself as she went to find Bob, but she couldn't help feeling a little bewildered and surprised by his brusque manner.

'What's going on with this young man?' Bob asked Patrick when he came into the theatre. 'Any sign of impending coma or shock syndrome? Is he panicking?'

Patrick shook his head. 'He's alert and coherent. He's been able to tell us how to contact his girlfriend. No sign of aortic tear or heart injury. I'm making a tentative diagnosis of lung bruising. I wanted your input.' He turned to Tilly, aware that the student nurse didn't have much experience of this kind of injury, and explained, 'These impact accidents often mean the victim inhales sharply and holds onto the air, and then a sharp blow to the chest, like Jed's had, can cause pressure to build up round the lungs, tearing open the superficial blood vessels.'

Bob nodded in agreement. 'Although Jed's in a lot of pain, he's not exhibiting the extreme panic that's often a sign of a chest injury involving the heart or aorta. Luckily he wasn't standing near a wall or another solid object when he was hit—that can make a hell of a mess of a body with multiple fractures or worse. We'll get him X-rayed and admitted to Surgical to have his respiration monitored and some pain relief administered.'

'Can you make those arrangements, Staff?' asked Patrick, his tone as remote as if he had hardly been introduced to Jandy.

Jandy went out with Tilly to book an X-ray and ring Surgical, a slow burn of annoyance beginning to flicker inside her at Patrick's manner. Perhaps she didn't know this man as well as she'd thought she did—he seemed to have reverted back to the rudeness he'd shown when she'd looked around the cottage. And yet…and yet only such a short time ago they had been in each other's arms and she'd been absolutely sure that he was her soul-mate. Surely the fiery intimacy they'd had together had meant more to him than just a casual fling? Then a little voice in her head whispered sadly, But didn't he warn you that he couldn't commit to anyone—that long-term relationships with him were not a possibility?

Tilly's breathless voice broke into her jangled thoughts. 'Wow—Dr Sinclair knows so much, doesn't he?' she said admiringly as they went to the desk.

'He's an experienced casualty officer,' commented Jandy rather tartly. 'He ought to know what he's talking about.'

Karen had just finished on the telephone. 'Right—that's done, then. I've managed to get hold of Jed's parents and his girlfriend, and they're coming in now. I haven't got any information yet on relatives of the two older men. They're both concussed and one's got a clean fracture of the right femur, but hopefully the police will dig something up.'

'Is the driver OK?' asked Jandy.

Karen pulled a face. 'Multiple fractures and a ruptured spleen so far—he's gone to Theatre. Looks like he's going to pay a heavy penalty for racing like that in a built-up area.'

'Pity he had to include the people hit by his car,' commented Bob. 'Have we time for a coffee? I'll collapse if I don't get some caffeine into my system.'

Jandy joined him in the little kitchen. 'Give me a strong one too, Bob,' she said. 'It's been a long day and we're not halfway through it yet.'

She sat down and lifted her feet onto another chair with a small sigh of relief, taking the chance to take the weight off them, like most casualty nurses did. She put her head back and closed her eyes for a minute, feeling an edgy irritation with the day, caused in no small part by Patrick, trying to pinpoint just what it might be that had made him so remote and formal. Perhaps, she reflected tiredly, she had it all wrong and was imagining his cold attitude towards her. After all, she couldn't expect the man to be all lovey-dovey with her in the hospital, for heaven's sake. She was expecting too much after their intimate time together in Scotland. She took a refreshing sip of the scalding coffee that Bob handed to her and felt slightly better.

At that moment Patrick came into the room, and she was struck suddenly by how tired and drawn he looked. He seemed to have aged a few years since they'd been together the day before. His father must be very ill, and in her selfishness she'd forgotten that he had things on his mind. He hadn't been deliberately rude to her—it was just that he was very worried.

She got up from the chair and poured him a cup of coffee.

'Hi, Patrick,' she said softly. 'I'm so sorry you had to leave suddenly. How is your father—is it very bad?'

Patrick took the coffee from her and shook his head. 'He's OK really,' he replied. For a second he looked at Jandy steadily, an unreadable expression in his eyes. 'Something happened, though—something that meant I couldn't stay any longer—but I don't want to talk about it just now.'

He gave no more information and Jandy frowned. It must be a private matter that he wouldn't want to discuss at work with everyone listening.

'Well, perhaps you'd like to do something to cheer you up?' she suggested brightly. 'There's a really good film on at the local cinema at the weekend. I could get a babysitter and we could have a meal after it perhaps. What do you say?'

She smiled at him, her beautiful eyes holding his. Inwardly Patrick groaned. He couldn't handle this. She was so beautiful and he longed to take her in his arms and kiss her lips, feel again her soft body next to his…bury his head in her sweet-smelling, silky hair. Then he thought of what he had learned so brutally about her attitude to him since they'd made glorious love to each other only thirty-six hours ago. He hardened his heart and swallowed a large draught of coffee. He couldn't allow himself to drift into a relationship again with someone whose regard for him was based on what she could get out of him. Both he and his precious Livy deserved more than that.

'Sorry,' he said tersely. 'I can't go out at the moment— a pretty full diary, I'm afraid.'

Jandy looked at him in surprise. 'You can't go out at all?'

His expression was cold, unreadable. 'Not possible at the moment—too much on.' He turned to Bob. 'Bob, I'd like your opinion on the old man with the broken femur—he's very shaky and I'm wondering if we've missed something.'

Bob nodded and they both went out discussing the old man's condition. Jandy took a deep breath, hardly able to believe Patrick's attitude towards her. What the hell was wrong—was it her? Had she been too demanding, too sure of herself, or was she just being hard on him? He looked different somehow—not the vibrant and energetic person he usually was. He probably needed a few days off from socialising and she was expecting too much from a man she knew was kind and considerate normally—after all, he'd come up to Scotland with her and been an enormous help and support. Perhaps when he'd finished work he'd get in touch with her. She shouldn't have pressured him in front of everyone. But somewhere deep inside her she had the horrible feeling that Patrick was moving away from her again. If he really loved her, he wouldn't have brushed her off like that. She gave a baffled sigh and went to answer the wall phone.

Patrick finished talking to Bob about the elderly patient and stood outside the small theatre for a second before he went to the locker room, watching Jandy walking back towards the main desk. He felt awful. He had wanted to make it plain to Jandy that they were no longer an item. In his bitter hurt at Jandy's deception he wanted to hurt her too, and he hated himself for it. He had seen the expression in her eyes when he'd told her he was too busy to go out with her, and it had twisted a knife in his heart, because he could almost swear that she looked heartbroken and bewildered, as if she really had loved him. But looks were deceptive, he told himself bitterly. He'd heard from her own mouth that what attracted her was his wealth and position.

'Damn it...damn her!' he muttered, slamming the locker door shut with a vicious bang and walking briskly out of the room.

As Jandy drove home that night she felt the ghastly replay of confusion and despair she'd experienced when Terry had abandoned her. Perhaps there was something about her, she thought savagely, that made her into a victim where men were concerned. And yet she could swear that Patrick was nothing like Terry. Even when she'd imagined she'd loved Terry, in her heart of hearts she'd known that he was a selfish man, someone who liked to be the centre of attention—extremely attractive with a spurious charm but devious in many ways. She recalled how he would have no compunction in taking days off if he wanted to go somewhere glamorous, phoning his office to say he was ill but assuring her that he would be working twice as hard to make up for his absence. She hadn't approved really, but when she'd been with him he'd had that charming knack of making her believe that he'd put himself out to be with her.

But Patrick was nothing like that. She'd worked closely with him, seen how dedicated, compassionate and kind he was. She couldn't believe that he really was the sort to have a one-night stand with anyone and deliberately hurt them.

Tears of desolation ran down her face as she drove to pick up Abigail, but she brushed them away fiercely, furious with herself for being so weak. Patrick Sinclair had lied to her—and she was worth more than that. She certainly wasn't going to spend years moping about any man again—life was too short to live wallowing in self-pity. She was glad, yes, glad that she'd found out about the rat now and not months later when she would probably have fallen for him hook, line and sinker. As it was, she was still in control of her feelings, wasn't she?

Unconsciously she tilted her chin in determination: Patrick was only going to be at Delford General for a short time until Sue came back from maternity leave. She would grit her teeth and work with him whatever the atmosphere between them.

Monday morning again and everywhere looked just the same—staff bustling about, Danny Smith on Reception laughing loudly at a joke Max had told him, a paramedic whistling cheerily in the corridor. Of course life went on, reflected Jandy gloomily. Just because her weekend had been sad and lonely, it didn't mean that the world outside mirrored her emotions.

'You look pretty shattered, Jandy,' remarked Bob. 'Had a busy weekend?'

What you mean is that I look absolutely awful, which could be because I hardly slept at all, thought Jandy, but she answered with a bright smile, 'Fairly busy. I've discovered moving house is very hard work and trying to box things up while an energetic four-year-old's helping you can be a little frustrating.'

She was well aware that Patrick was very close to her, leafing through a medical journal, but she didn't look at him. She wouldn't let him get to her—she wouldn't!

'Shall I go and take the first on the list?' she asked Bob. 'Monday mornings mean hundreds of patients with hang-overs from the weekend, and worse!'

She went to Reception and took the top card in the box from the pile of triaged patients.

'Harry Leyton?' she called out.

A large man wearing overalls and boots came forward, holding a dirty handkerchief over his finger.

'Fine start to the day this is!' he commented, sitting down in the cubicle that Jandy had taken him to. 'I think I've taken off the top of my finger.'

'Let me see,' said Jandy, unwinding the material from his finger and blanching slightly when she saw that the finger had been cut through the nail bed to the bone. 'How on earth did you do this?'

'Pushing a bill through a letter box. The lid smacked down on my finger and I tried to pull my finger out. That was a mistake—it held my finger like a vice.'

Jandy grimaced in sympathy. 'Not what you expect when you post a letter. Now, I'm going to wash it very, very gently—we've got to make sure it's clean—and then I'm going to bind it up to stop it bleeding.'

'What about stitching it? Won't that make it heal quicker?' the man asked.

'There isn't much skin there to stitch. I think it will just have to heal over by itself. It'll probably take two or three weeks.'

Harry groaned. 'I'm not going to be able to do much joinery with a hand like this, am I?' He shook his large fleshy face gloomily. 'Well, that's ruined my day, I can tell you. How can I look after my family if I can't work? I've got a big contract on as well with a building firm...'

'I'm sorry, Harry,' said Jandy as she cleaned and bandaged the injury. 'It's very bad luck—but it will heal if you don't try and use it too much.'

He nodded and sighed. 'Maybe—but this is the first

big job I've had in an age. It was going to set me up a bit, this was.'

Jandy watched Harry lumber off, feeling intensely sorry for him. She knew what it was like to be hard up—but at least she had a regular job. Her heart might be broken, but as long as she could look after Abigail and keep a roof over their heads she mustn't complain.

She went to the central desk to put the patient's case notes on the computer, brushing past Patrick who was writing something up on the whiteboard. He turned to look at her slim figure with her back to him as she sat in front of the screen. Bob was sitting by her, just finishing a telephone conversation. He put down the phone and turned to Jandy.

'You still look a bit bushed,' he said. 'You wouldn't fancy having a drink with a few of us after work, would you?'

Out of the corner of her eye she was aware that Patrick was watching her, but with an abrupt movement he rose from his chair and strode out of the room. She gave an inward shrug. She had to put Patrick Sinclair out of her mind.

She smiled ruefully at Bob. 'I'm terribly busy at the moment, Bob. Moving house in a few days means every hour after work is taken up with packing and sorting. It'll be some time before I can take time off.'

He nodded affably. 'Just a thought. Hope the move goes OK.'

Jandy turned to go back to Reception and on the way passed Patrick. He caught her arm, a grim expression on his face.

'So you're going out with Bob now, are you?' he said stonily to her.

She stared at him in amazement, lost for speech. What

was this man like? But her heart started pounding at his touch, a kind of excitement building up in her that he was at least communicating with her.

'I beg your pardon?' she said tartly with a raised eyebrow. 'I don't know what you're talking about. Bob asked me out for a drink with some of the others, but for your information I declined—not that it's any business of yours!'

Then, with a withering look of scorn, she walked away from him.

Patrick clenched his fists in his pockets. He hadn't known it would hurt this much, listening to another man asking Jandy out. He hadn't realised that the thought of her with anyone else would be like a knife turning in his stomach. He sat at the desk and looked down at his hands, seeing the golden wedding band he still had on his ring finger. Rachel would forever have a special place in his heart—but that was in another life. Now he knew that whatever he had found out about Jandy's reason for going out with him, it was she who dominated all his thoughts at the moment—and he was eaten up by jealousy, unable to do anything about it.

CHAPTER TEN

'I THINK we're all done, love. The van's empty now, so we'll be off!'

The genial removal men gave a wave and went off down the path, the door of the cottage banged shut and Jandy and Lydia flopped down on the sofa.

'Thank God!' exclaimed Lydia. 'We're in at last! And it looks lovely after all the hard work you've put in, Jandy, painting and scrubbing. I'm sorry you had to do it all.'

'Oh, I quite enjoyed it. There's something satisfying about seeing a result. Anyway, you've been doing your stuff with Mum in Scotland for a week. You say she's doing really well?'

'It's amazing how's she's improved, and Bertie's coming home next week.'

There was the sound of pattering feet on the stairs and Abigail ran across the room, eyes alight with joy. She was so precious, thought Jandy, so full of life and exuberance. It made everything worthwhile, and even helped to subdue the unhappiness of the situation between Patrick and herself.

'Mummy, Lydia, come and look at my room—it's got

lots of pictures up of flowers and fairies and little animals! I love it!'

'We'll come in a minute, pet. Just let Mummy and I have a little sit-down—we're exhausted,' begged Lydia.

'Well, I want to show Livy my room soon,' declared Abigail. 'Can we ask her to come round? You said she could come when we were all moved in.'

She looked pleadingly at Jandy, and Lydia grinned. 'What a good idea. Livy's Patrick's little girl, isn't she? Why don't we have a small house-warming party with Livy and Patrick? Give them a call, Jandy. After all, it was Patrick who mentioned the cottage was to let and he hasn't seen it transformed yet.'

Jandy felt her cheeks redden, suddenly at a complete loss as to what to say. The last thing she wanted was to see Patrick. In the future she supposed it was inevitable they'd meet in the little village as they lived so near each other, but at the moment her feelings were too raw, still smarting from his incredible behaviour a week ago. They had seen each other in the hospital, of course, worked on the same patients sometimes, but had barely exchanged words. It was horrible, but she was going to stick it out until Patrick left in a few months. Sometimes she thought he was about to say something to her—but so far she had skilfully avoided entering into any conversation with him. If he hadn't the basic politeness to tell her why he didn't want to pursue their relationship then she didn't want to have anything to do with him.

'He's on holiday at the moment,' Jandy said quickly, glad that she didn't have to lie. 'I know he's taken a few days off, so we'll have to wait until he comes back.'

Abigail's little face fell, then she said resolutely, 'I'm going to send Livy an invitation. Will you help me to write it, Mummy? I'll go and get my crayons.'

'I must say I can't wait to see the guy,' said Lydia chattily as Abigail raced upstairs for her crayons. She opened a bottle of sparkling wine to celebrate their move. 'Mum is in ecstasies about him—says he's got everything! I thought perhaps I'd see him round here before I have to fly off again on Wednesday.' She handed a glass of wine to Jandy. 'Cheers! Here's to happy times. By the way, has Patrick told you why he had to leave Scotland so quickly last week? And before I got to see him too!'

Jandy took a sip of wine and twirled her glass, watching the bubbles rise to the surface. 'Er…no, he hasn't mentioned it, actually.'

Lydia raised her eyebrows in surprise at her twin. 'Why on earth not? I must say, it's the first thing I'd ask him. You were really worried about what had happened to his father, weren't you?'

'I did try and find out but he said he didn't want to discuss it in front of everyone at the hospital—and I can't say I blame him.'

'But you must have had times alone with him surely—even after work perhaps?'

Jandy was silent for a second and Lydia looked at her curiously, then she put her glass down and came over to Jandy and took her hand, saying softly, 'You can't fool me, darling…I'm not your twin sister for nothing. Something's wrong, isn't it? Have you had a row?'

Jandy swallowed. 'Not really…well, sort of…' She shrugged, her eyes a little too bright, and said with a weary half-smile, 'No use keeping anything from you, is there? The truth is, Lydia, I don't know what went wrong. We were getting along beautifully in Scotland. It was wonderful, and I really thought he liked me a lot—there was no sign of anything wrong. And then...and then when I came back from the shops after you'd arrived, he'd just vanished! And...'

She stopped and wandered over to the window, gazing out at the little garden and the mansion house beyond it where Patrick lived.

'And what?' prompted Lydia. 'His note implied that it was something to do with home, didn't it? Nothing to do with you and him.'

Jandy whipped round from the window and burst out, 'But it must have been something about me—don't you see? We were so very close on the night we'd come back from seeing Mum in hospital. I...I thought we'd made each other very happy. It all seemed absolutely perfect. And then...without a word he vanishes and since then he's barely exchanged two words with me—except to be curt and rude. I just can't understand it.'

'Poor darling,' whispered Lydia, hugging her sister. 'I can't believe it is anything to do with you. It must be something much deeper than that—some background worry that's making him like this. Perhaps when he's returned from holiday he'll have sorted it out and things will get back to normal.'

'I don't think so, sis. I've come to the conclusion that he just doesn't want any sort of commitment and he's frightened I'll be too possessive—something like that. You know, he still wears his wedding ring and perhaps that's a sign that he hasn't let go of the past yet.' Jandy drained her wineglass, put it down on the table and said sadly, 'Whatever it is, I'm damn well not going to make another mistake and fall for someone who can toss me aside so easily.'

'I don't want anyone to hurt you again either— I just can't believe that this man is another Terry, though. You know, Mum's a pretty good judge of character and she never liked Terry, even before he deserted you—but Patrick Sinclair's a different story. She really was impressed with him.'

Jandy gave a sudden laugh. 'Oh, well, I'm going to forget about the rat anyway. Tell me about this dishy new pilot you've met. Are you smitten?'

Lydia grinned. 'Let's finish this bottle, and I'll tell you the whole story.'

It was a cold night with a wintry feel and Jandy had made up a log fire with apple wood and it sent out a lovely fresh smell and warmed the room beautifully. Jandy thought how cosy it was as she snuggled down on the sofa, ready to switch on the TV and watch a talent show. She had looked forward all week to a quiet Saturday evening. Abigail was already in bed and Jandy was nibbling at some smoked-salmon sandwiches she'd made for herself as Lydia had flown off again on some exotic flight or other.

She gave a jump of irritation when there was a knock at the front door then wondered rather fearfully if she ought to open it when it was so dark outside. She called out, 'Who is it?'

'It's Bob—Bob Thoms. Just dropping in a little house-warming present from us all, but if it's not convenient…'

'Hi, Bob, how sweet of you to bring a present. Do come in,' she said, opening the door.

'Well…if it's OK,' he said. 'I'm just on my way to meet up with our shift and they asked me to drop these off.' He handed her an enormous bunch of flowers. He looked around the room. 'This is very nice—did you say it belonged to Patrick?'

'Well, it's on his father's estate and he wanted to let it and I was desperate to get somewhere. I was very lucky. What about a drink?'

Bob shot a look at his watch and shook his head. 'I'm only staying for a minute as I promised I'd pick Tilly up, so I'd better be on my way.'

'Well, thanks to all of you for these gorgeous flowers. It's really sweet of you.'

She was interrupted by another knock on the front door. She smiled at Bob and said wryly, 'You wait ages for someone to call and then two come along at once!'

She opened the door and looked with astonishment into Patrick's eyes as he stood before her. A flicker of something very like longing and distress seemed to cross his face before his expression changed and became hard and remote again.

Oh, Patrick, whispered Jandy to herself. Why has it come to this? Why do you seem to dislike me so much? From love to hate so very quickly!

She might have been determined to put the man out of her mind, but when she saw him in the flesh—his glorious sexy body, wide shouldered, slim hipped, dark hair plastered wetly round his head from the rain—her resolution slipped somewhat.

Patrick's eyes flicked to Bob standing behind her.

'I didn't realise that you and Bob were having an evening together,' he remarked brusquely. In her heightened state Jandy detected a kind of sarcasm in the remark. 'I won't be long, though,' he added. 'I just came to see that you'd moved in OK—and if there was anything that needed doing. We always make sure there are no problems with our new tenants.' He said that smoothly as if to underline that there was nothing special about him coming to see her.

Jandy stood stock still, numb with shock and still holding the bouquet of flowers. 'No…no, thank you. Everything's quite all right.'

'Well,' said Bob easily, oblivious to the atmosphere between Jandy and Patrick. 'I'll be off now anyway. Nice to see you, Patrick. See you both on Monday, I suppose!'

He opened the front door and Jandy called out as he left, 'Thank you so much for the flowers—they're really beautiful.'

'Glad you like them!' he called, disappearing down the little path and getting into his car. Jandy watched him go then turned round slowly to face Patrick, who was still standing by the fireplace. He looked drop-dead handsome, but weary and grey faced, as if he hadn't been sleeping too well.

'Is that all you wanted to see me about—whether everything was all right?' she asked tersely after a short silence.

'Yes…yes, that's all.' He folded his arms and looked down at the floor for a second as if gathering his thoughts, before raising his head again and lasering her with those deep blue eyes.

'So you and Bob are seeing each other after all?' he enquired smoothly.

'I've no idea what you mean. He kindly brought some flowers round tonight as a house-warming present—although it's nothing to do with you actually,' she said bitingly, nearly adding, As you seem to have lost interest in me. But she couldn't bring herself to utter the finality of those words.

Patrick shrugged. 'Well, I suppose old Bob has a bit of money stashed away—he's only got himself to support after all, so I expect he's perfect for you.'

For a second Jandy couldn't believe she'd heard him correctly then she said slowly, 'I beg your pardon? Are you saying I only going out with men if they've got some money?'

'It seems to make sense to me. The guy drives an expensive car, goes on luxury holidays. It would suit you down to the ground…'

A sudden blind fury overtook Jandy. How could he be so cruel, so unkind? 'How dare you?' she said in a dangerously quiet voice. 'I cannot believe what you just said, and I can't think what I've done to justify you making such a horrible remark. Not that it matters, but that bouquet was from the casualty team and not just Bob. Would you get out now? I don't want to see you in this house again. I may be renting it from your father, but from now on, keep your distance!'

She marched to the door and held it open, allowing the freezing air to come into the room, and Patrick walked slowly past her, only turning at the last moment so that he was standing in front of her.

'It hurts to be told the truth, doesn't it, Jandy?' he said softly, and walked away into the night. Jandy flung herself onto the sofa and cried until there were no tears left.

Patrick walked home miserably, almost revelling in the rain that lashed into him—a kind of punishment, he thought, for being so unbelievably brutal to Jandy. How could he say such lacerating words to a woman he knew now he loved?

He'd gone round that night on the pretext of asking Jandy if everything was to her satisfaction after her move because he couldn't bear to let the situation between them go on any longer. He had been going to try and have it out with her—to ask her to tell him honestly if money was one of the things that had attracted her to him. He desperately wanted to get back to where they'd been before and could hardly credit that he'd heard her say that his money and status were what she was interested in. But when he'd seen Bob there he'd felt it was too late. She'd moved on already, and he couldn't bear the thought of her with another man. So much for commitment, he thought bitterly, turning into the drive of Easterleigh and hunching up his jacket against the rain.

Jandy woke the next morning with a dull headache, finding it hard to find the energy to be upbeat for Abigail, who begged to be allowed to deliver the note she'd written to Livy, asking her round for tea.

'Can we walk round to Livy's house, Mummy, and take the invitation? They're probably back from their holiday. Please, please, please! It's not raining!' Abigail looked hopefully at her mother.

'Not at the moment, darling. I've got a lot of urgent things to do.'

Abigail pouted. 'What urgent things? You've never got time for anything with me!'

Those words stung. As a single parent Jandy was always conscious of the fact that her time with her little girl was limited and she did her best to make up for it at the weekends, but today she felt utterly drained, unable to respond to Abigail's entreaties.

'Perhaps later on, pet. Let me do the ironing first.'

There was the sound of footsteps coming up the path and then the front door opened and Lydia came into the room. Jandy felt her heart lift a little. How wonderful that her sister was back—things never seemed as bad when she was around.

'Oh, Lydia, darling—I didn't expect you back yet!'

Jandy flung her arms round her sister, never more happy to see her. She needed her sister's bracing fun and understanding more than ever, although she was not going to tell her about the episode with Patrick the night before. It was no good going over that horrible conversation again.

'Ah, it's nice to be wanted.' Lydia laughed. 'The flight out to Australia was cancelled when we got to Amsterdam and so I've got a few days off. Hallelujah!' She turned to her little niece. 'And how is my adorable little Abigail? By the way, I've got something for you!'

She delved into a bag and Abigail fluttered excitedly round her until Lydia produced a little doll wearing a flight attendant's uniform with a bag that held changes of clothes.

'Ooh, she's lovely. Thank you very, very much!' exclaimed Abigail, prancing around the room and waving the doll about. 'She looks like you and I'm going to call her Lucy! This is something else I can show to Livy!'

Jandy groaned and caught her sister's eye. 'She's still keen to see Livy. I've told her very possibly she might, but only possibly, later! Now, how about a cup of coffee?'

She and Lydia went into the kitchen, talking nineteen to the dozen as they always did when they got together. Abigail looked after them and sighed then, clutching the little doll, she went quietly out of the front door and down the path.

'Look, Jandy, she can't have gone far. You know what? I bet she's toddled off to show Livy that doll all by herself.'

The strain of the past few frantic minutes when Jandy and Lydia had searched the house and garden for Abigail after discovering she was missing was beginning to tell. They both looked fraught.

'It's a possibility,' Jandy admitted. 'I should have taken more notice of her when she pleaded to see Livy—I was far too vague. Let's go and see if she's made her way to the hall. Oh, God, I hope she's all right.'

They ran out of the garden and up the road to the gates of Easterleigh. The drive stretched a long way before them, dripping bare trees on either side, a slight bend halfway up meaning that only half the house was visible.

'Lord, look how far away it is—a hell of a way for a little girl to go by herself,' whispered Lydia.

'If she sets her mind on something, she'll do it,' said Jandy wryly. 'Come on, let's run!'

When they came to the curve in the drive it divided into two with no indication as to which way led to the hall. They looked at each other in exasperation.

Then Jandy said, 'Good job there's two of us. You go that way, I'll go this!'

The dogs were making an almighty row, thought Patrick as he strode through the woodland, taking stock of the trees that needed felling and the fences that had broken down by the river. They were probably after rabbits again—there were enough of them scampering all over the place. Winter had arrived. There was a crust of frost on the ground from overnight and it was cold and damp. In four weeks it would be Christmas.

A wave of depression came over him as he reflected that Livy wanted a Christmas party and the house to be decorated with a huge Christmas tree in the hall. Patrick smiled grimly to himself. He didn't feel like celebrating at the moment. Two weeks ago he had been full of plans for Jandy and Abigail—and the sister, of course, whom he'd never met—joining them for Christmas Day and having a wonderful traditional time. How his father would love that—filling the house with laughter and children's excitement. Now he would have to force himself to enjoy the festivities for Livy's sake.

A sudden noise in the woods caught Patrick's attention. He could hear a woman's voice calling and the dogs sent up a new cacophony of barking.

'Rusty! Lightning! Here, boys! Come here at once!' he shouted.

A crashing through the undergrowth and they bounded in front of him obediently. He bent down to ruffle their heads and then heard the woman's voice again, high and frightened.

'Abigail! Abigail, darling—are you there?'

'What the…?'

Patrick pushed his way through the bushes and small trees and nearly fell over Jandy standing in a little clearing. She looked round when she heard the sound of crunching footsteps behind her, her eyes alight with hope. Then she saw it was Patrick and her expression changed to one of despair.

He looked at her distraught face. 'What on earth's wrong? What are you doing here?'

'It…it's Abigail…' she gasped. 'She's wandered off. We think she may have come to see Livy and show her a doll my sister brought her. She may have left the drive and taken a wrong turning.' Jandy looked around wildly. 'I don't know where to start looking… Oh, God, if anything's happened to her…'

Patrick put his hands on her shoulders. 'Don't worry. If she's anywhere in the vicinity, we'll find her. We'll make our way towards the house through the woods. If we haven't found her by then I'll get the staff together and we'll all search for her.' He put his hand under her chin and tilted her face towards his. His expression was gentle, un-flustered. 'Pecker up!' He turned to the dogs. 'Come on, boys! Seek and find with me!'

The dogs darted in and out of the undergrowth and Patrick grabbed Jandy's hand to steady her as they made their way along a narrow path, both of them shouting Abigail's name then stopping to listen in case she replied. After a few minutes they heard the dogs whining and Patrick's grip on Jandy's hand tightened.

'They've seen something,' he said. 'They always whine when they see something strange. We're coming to another clearing now.'

The path opened up into a small clearing with a little summer house in the middle. Sitting on the step to the door was Abigail, playing with her doll. She looked up as she heard the two adults approach.

'Hello!' she said brightly. 'I've found this little house to play in!'

Jandy took a deep breath and went and sat beside her. 'Why did you go out without telling Lydia or me?' she asked the child gently.

''Cos I knew you wouldn't take me to see Livy for ages and ages—you're always talking to Lydia when she comes home.'

'Abigail,' said Jandy in a very stern voice, 'I want you to promise that you'll never ever go out again without telling Mummy. I've been very worried about you. Lydia, Patrick and I have been searching for you—do you hear?'

Abigail nodded. 'I'm glad you found me. I lost my way but I wasn't frightened.'

Jandy's eyes met Patrick's and she got up and said quietly to him, 'Thank you for helping me. We won't trespass on your land any more.'

'Perhaps it would be a good idea for you and Abigail to come to the house and she can show Livy her doll?' He spoke diffidently, as if he didn't really mind one way or the other, but his eyes never left her.

'I don't think in the circumstances...' Jandy began stiffly.

'Oh, please, Mummy! Just for a little minute!' Abigail ran to her mother and put her arms round Jandy's legs. 'I'll be a good girl for you!'

Jandy flicked a glance at Patrick and said resignedly, 'Well, just for a few minutes—if that's all right with Patrick.'

They started to make their way down the path and came to the drive again, this time much nearer the house. At the same time a figure appeared out of the woodland on the opposite side.

'Lydia!' called Jandy, running over to her. 'Lydia, it's OK! We've found Abigail!'

'Oh, thank God!' Lydia ran up to the little girl and flung her arms round her. 'Don't give us such a fright again, darling, will you?'

Patrick stood watching them, a slight look of puzzlement on his face, and Jandy drew Lydia towards him.

'This is my sister, Lydia,' she said. 'She came up to Scotland just before you left, but you didn't meet each other.'

He looked at the two sisters incredulously. They were incredibly alike, although he could tell there were subtle differences—Jandy waas slightly taller and slimmer than Lydia, her hair a little fairer.

'Pleased to meet you, Lydia,' he said at last. 'I didn't realise you and your sister were twins, Jandy.' He frowned for a second. 'So you came up to Scotland when we were there?'

'I managed to get a flight up to Inverness when I'd come back from Australia and took a taxi straight to my mother's house. I wanted it to be a surprise for them—they didn't know I was coming. I was sorry to miss you.'

They started to walk towards the house, Patrick silent and thoughtful, then he stopped suddenly and said, 'Did you arrive while Jandy was at the shops?'

'Yes—you'd gone for a walk and she'd popped out to get some basics in before she flew home in the evening.' Lydia looked reproachfully at him. 'Actually, she was amazed when she returned and found you'd left. We couldn't really understand it!'

Patrick was silent for a moment, and just then a small figure appeared in the doorway of the big house. She gave a shriek of surprise and ran up to them.

'Abigail!' she cried happily. 'You've come to see me! Can I show her my pony, Daddy, now she's here?'

'You can, sweetheart—but first of all take Abigail and her auntie into the house and ask Sheena to get everyone a coffee. Jandy and I will be in soon—I just want to have a word with her.'

Lydia took the two children's hands and walked ahead with them, pausing very briefly to give Jandy a significant wink. For an unaccountable reason Jandy's heart began to thud uncomfortably against her ribs. What could Patrick possibly have to say to her? She had nothing to say to him whatsoever after his incredible rudeness the evening before. She was grateful for his help in finding Abigail, but that didn't mean they could be friends again, did it?

He took her arm and drew her to the side of the house then turned her round to face him, his hands holding her arms. She could feel their warmth through her sweater, their strength as he gripped her. He looked down at her with an extraordinary expression of disbelief and sadness.

'Jandy...' he began haltingly. 'I don't know how to tell you this...how to start, and it sounds utterly incredible, but I've made the most terrible mistake I think I've ever made in my life. I don't know if you can ever forgive me.'

Jandy looked at him scornfully. 'What do you mean— the mistake of being rude to me with no justification whatsoever? Why should I forgive you?'

He put his finger on her mouth. 'Give me a minute, sweetheart.'

Sweetheart? Who did he think he was kidding? After what he'd said to her, that was the last thing she was—

'Of course I should never have said those things, but I made a terrible error when I was in Scotland. I jumped to the wrong conclusion. I thought I heard you say something to the effect that you were glad I had plenty of money and that it would be great to be called Lady Sinclair…'

Jandy gazed at him, open-mouthed. 'That is so ridiculous,' she said slowly. 'How on earth could you think I would even think that, let alone say it?'

'I don't know,' he said miserably. 'I should have come into the room and questioned what I thought you said, but I was horrified and taken aback.'

A gleam of understanding began to appear in Jandy's eyes. 'You thought you heard me say those things—but it wasn't me, was it?'

He shook his head. 'It was your sister. I only saw her from the back and she was talking to your mother. Of course I hadn't realised she'd come up—I didn't even know you were twins. Now I know she was just joking, but when I heard her make those comments it took me back to shortly after Rachel died.'

'Why was that?' asked Jandy, frowning.

'I was distraught after her death, of course, feeling terrible guilt that I had caused it.' He looked at Jandy wryly. 'To lose the one you love after a silly quarrel means you never forgive yourself. On the rebound I became engaged to a girl at work. I hardly knew what I was doing, but I was lonely and she was very, very persistent. I found myself getting more and more involved with her. I suppose I thought I loved her.'

Jandy watched him intently, hardly able to believe her ears. 'So what happened?' she said, her eyes large with sympathy.

'I found she had been using my name to do all kinds of things—buying stuff on credit, getting the best seats in theatres on the strength of me being the Honourable Patrick

Sinclair—but worst of all I'd heard her needlessly shouting at Livy, telling her off for nothing at all.'

'And you realised that you could be landing little Livy with another stepmother from hell, like you had?'

He nodded. 'When I found out I was enraged. She actually admitted it was my connections that attracted her—she didn't love me and she wasn't all that keen on children.' He laughed grimly. 'Needless to say, as soon as we split up she found some other poor man to fasten onto—someone much older who had real wealth.'

'A lucky escape,' murmured Jandy.

'I'd been a fool. She was the sort of girl I would never normally have taken out, but after the trauma of Rachel's death I don't think I knew what I was doing. In fact, I soon realised it was a relief to be rid of her. But it made me terrified of making the same mistake again.'

Jandy looked at him stonily, pushing any sympathetic thoughts to the back of her head. 'You thought I was another girl out for the main chance, then?'

He took her shoulders and pulled her towards him, and she found herself allowing him to do that, to press his chest to hers. She felt the thud of his heart as they stood hip to hip, and he looked down at her with burning blue eyes.

'Of course you're not,' he said fiercely. 'You're nothing at all like her. Meeting you seemed almost too good to be true. I think I loved you almost the first time I saw you. I knew within five minutes of talking to you that I wanted to kiss you...but you had an unhappy past too and I was wary of commitment.' He sighed and shook his head. 'How can one guy be so stupid? And how could I have been so cruel to you over these past few weeks?'

Jandy's eyes searched his face, and she whispered, 'And if you hadn't found out it was my sister who'd made those flippant remarks I wouldn't have ever got an apology, then?'

'I haven't stopped thinking about you since I left Scotland—not for a single minute. That was why I came round last night. I was desperate to set things straight between us. Then I found Bob already ensconced there, and said things I didn't mean—just to hurt you, I suppose.'

He paused for a moment and bent his head to hers, whispering in a broken voice, 'But I didn't mean it, my darling, I didn't mean it. I felt awful as I was saying those horrible things...'

Jandy pulled away from him and stepped back, folding her arms and looking at him wryly.

'So where does that leave us, Patrick? Back where we were, in no-man's land, loving each other but not being too committed—a kind of halfway house?'

He shook his head vehemently and drew her towards him again, saying with a catch in his voice, 'Sweetheart, no half-measures this time. I'm not going to risk letting you get away. I love you so much, darling—can you believe that? Can you ever forgive me for what I said?'

A little bubble of happiness seemed to explode somewhere in the region of Jandy's stomach. Was she dreaming? Had Patrick really said he loved her?

'Say you love me again then,' she demanded.

'I love you, adore you, worship you...'

Jandy burst out laughing. 'OK, OK—that's enough! I forgive you.'

He looked at her solemnly for a moment. 'Perhaps this will convince you that I mean what I say, Jandy...show you that the past really is behind us both. No more guilt, no more distrust.' He looked down at his left hand and spread out his fingers then pulled off his wedding ring and slipped it into his pocket. 'I shall never forget Rachel or the love I had for her—but now there's room on that hand for another ring. I want you to marry me, for us to spend the rest of our lives together. What do you say to that?'

For answer she wound her arms round his neck and pulled his face down to hers, then pressed her soft mouth to his, crushing herself to his hard body.

'Do I take that as a "yes" then?' he said with a grin after a few minutes. Then he tucked her hand under his arm. 'And now let's go and tell our adorable daughters that from now on they're going to have a mummy and a daddy to look after them.'

The front lawn was bathed in warm sunlight and the summer smell of new-mown grass was sweet in the balmy air. There was a low murmur of voices from the little congregation sitting on the chairs before a small altar, with two pedestals of huge vases of tumbling pink roses and meadowsweet on either side. A slight warm breeze rustled the leaves of the beautiful oaks that formed a background circle round the lawn.

In the front row sat Patrick's father in his wheelchair and Jandy's mother and Bertie, smiling and chatting to each other. There was an excited air of expectancy and in a corner was the soft sound of a small keyboard organ being played by Sheena, the housekeeper.

Standing in front of them all were the tall figures of Patrick and his brother, and as the music changed to the joyous Bridal March they turned round to watch Jandy coming down the steps of the beautiful old house, her slim figure in a cream sheath dress and accompanied by her sister in pale green silk. Behind them, with little giggles of nervousness, came Abigail and Livy, the two little girls proudly holding Jandy's train, wearing full-length cream dresses with pink sashes.

As they all came towards Patrick he smiled very tenderly at them and held his hands out to his bride to lead her to his side.

'Hello, all my beautiful girls,' he murmured. 'What a lovely way to start our wedding day!'

And Jandy was smiling too, a radiant, dazzling smile, and there were tears running down her face—but this time they were tears of happiness. Married life with her darling Patrick was about to begin.

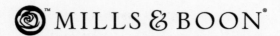

JUNE 2010 HARDBACK TITLES

ROMANCE

Marriage: To Claim His Twins	Penny Jordan
The Royal Baby Revelation	Sharon Kendrick
Under the Spaniard's Lock and Key	Kim Lawrence
Sweet Surrender with the Millionaire	Helen Brooks
The Virgin's Proposition	Anne McAllister
Scandal: His Majesty's Love-Child	Annie West
Bride in a Gilded Cage	Abby Green
Innocent in the Italian's Possession	Janette Kenny
The Master of Highbridge Manor	Susanne James
The Power of the Legendary Greek	Catherine George
Miracle for the Girl Next Door	Rebecca Winters
Mother of the Bride	Caroline Anderson
What's A Housekeeper To Do?	Jennie Adams
Tipping the Waitress with Diamonds	Nina Harrington
Saving Cinderella!	Myrna Mackenzie
Their Newborn Gift	Nikki Logan
The Midwife and the Millionaire	Fiona McArthur
Knight on the Children's Ward	Carol Marinelli

HISTORICAL

Rake Beyond Redemption	Anne O'Brien
A Thoroughly Compromised Lady	Bronwyn Scott
In the Master's Bed	Blythe Gifford

MEDICAL™

From Single Mum to Lady	Judy Campbell
Children's Doctor, Shy Nurse	Molly Evans
Hawaiian Sunset, Dream Proposal	Joanna Neil
Rescued: Mother and Baby	Anne Fraser

0510 Gen Std LP

MILLS & BOON

JUNE 2010 LARGE PRINT TITLES

ROMANCE

The Wealthy Greek's Contract Wife	Penny Jordan
The Innocent's Surrender	Sara Craven
Castellano's Mistress of Revenge	Melanie Milburne
The Italian's One-Night Love-Child	Cathy Williams
Cinderella on His Doorstep	Rebecca Winters
Accidentally Expecting!	Lucy Gordon
Lights, Camera…Kiss the Boss	Nikki Logan
Australian Boss: Diamond Ring	Jennie Adams

HISTORICAL

The Rogue's Disgraced Lady	Carole Mortimer
A Marriageable Miss	Dorothy Elbury
Wicked Rake, Defiant Mistress	Ann Lethbridge

MEDICAL™

Snowbound: Miracle Marriage	Sarah Morgan
Christmas Eve: Doorstep Delivery	Sarah Morgan
Hot-Shot Doc, Christmas Bride	Joanna Neil
Christmas at Rivercut Manor	Gill Sanderson
Falling for the Playboy Millionaire	Kate Hardy
The Surgeon's New-Year Wedding Wish	Laura Iding

0610 Gen Std HB

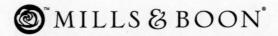

JULY 2010 HARDBACK TITLES

ROMANCE

A Night, A Secret...A Child	Miranda Lee
His Untamed Innocent	Sara Craven
The Greek's Pregnant Lover	Lucy Monroe
The Mélendez Forgotten Marriage	Melanie Milburne
Sensible Housekeeper, Scandalously Pregnant	Jennie Lucas
The Bride's Awakening	Kate Hewitt
The Devil's Heart	Lynn Raye Harris
The Good Greek Wife?	Kate Walker
Propositioned by the Billionaire	Lucy King
Unbuttoned by Her Maverick Boss	Natalie Anderson
Australia's Most Eligible Bachelor	Margaret Way
The Bridesmaid's Secret	Fiona Harper
Cinderella: Hired by the Prince	Marion Lennox
The Sheikh's Destiny	Melissa James
Vegas Pregnancy Surprise	Shirley Jump
The Lionhearted Cowboy Returns	Patricia Thayer
Dare She Date the Dreamy Doc?	Sarah Morgan
Neurosurgeon ... and Mum!	Kate Hardy

HISTORICAL

Vicar's Daughter to Viscount's Lady	Louise Allen
Chivalrous Rake, Scandalous Lady	Mary Brendan
The Lord's Forced Bride	Anne Herries

MEDICAL™

Dr Drop-Dead Gorgeous	Emily Forbes
Her Brooding Italian Surgeon	Fiona Lowe
A Father for Baby Rose	Margaret Barker
Wedding in Darling Downs	Leah Martyn

0610 Gen Std LP

⊚™ MILLS & BOON®

JULY 2010 LARGE PRINT TITLES

ROMANCE

Greek Tycoon, Inexperienced Mistress	Lynne Graham
The Master's Mistress	Carole Mortimer
The Andreou Marriage Arrangement	Helen Bianchin
Untamed Italian, Blackmailed Innocent	Jacqueline Baird
Outback Bachelor	Margaret Way
The Cattleman's Adopted Family	Barbara Hannay
Oh-So-Sensible Secretary	Jessica Hart
Housekeeper's Happy-Ever-After	Fiona Harper

HISTORICAL

One Unashamed Night	Sophia James
The Captain's Mysterious Lady	Mary Nichols
The Major and the Pickpocket	Lucy Ashford

MEDICAL™

Posh Doc, Society Wedding	Joanna Neil
The Doctor's Rebel Knight	Melanie Milburne
A Mother for the Italian's Twins	Margaret McDonagh
Their Baby Surprise	Jennifer Taylor
New Boss, New-Year Bride	Lucy Clark
Greek Doctor Claims His Bride	Margaret Barker

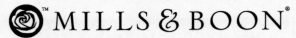

MONKLANDS.   9-30 . Am .